DARK SECRETS

Aidan Lucid

© Copyright Aidan Lucid 2023

Published by Aidan Lucid 2023

Book design by Aidan Lucid

Front cover illustration by Smstudioinc (https://www.fiverr.com/smstudioinc)

Back cover by Cherilyn Yap

ISBN: 978-1-7391598-4-9

ISBN: 978-1-7391598-5-6

ISBN: 978-1-7391598-6-3

For more information about Aidan Lucid and his books, go to www.aidanlucidauthor.com

Acknowledgements

I'd like to thank the following:

Beta readers: Simonadarkthrill, Dawn Robinson, and Manusri for their excellent input.

Megan Openshaw for her fantastic editing work.

Smstudioinc for producing yet another superb cover.

Cherilyn Yap for the back cover.

God for giving me the gift of writing.

And finally, you, for purchasing this novella.

Thanks, and God bless you all.

BOOKS BY THIS AUTHOR

The Zargothian Saga Series

The Lost Son (Second Edition)

Deadly Pursuits (Summer 2024)

When Worlds Collide (Winter 2025)

Jasper's Christmas Adventure (Winter 2026)

Hopps Town Series

The Scavenger

Unlucky Charm

Dark Secrets

Lurking Beasts (Summer 2024)

Stand-Alone Fiction

The Perfect Christmas Gift (short story)

A Beast Within (October 2023)

Praise for the Hopps Town Series

"*The Scavenger* is a nail-biting story with lots of nail-biting excitement. It was hard to put down. 4.5 fun spooky stars!"

> \- Priscilla Bettis, author

"A coming-of-age story with heavy allegorical elements, the themes Lucid explores are important and timely. Blending fantastical elements with relatable relationships, authentic dialogue, and common struggles too often left undiscussed, this book does what YA literature should always strive for—educate, entertain, and inspire."

> \- Self-Publishing Review

"A fun YA horror, with a fast pace and a mystery to uncover."

> \- Well Worth a Read blog

"Lots of people have played with the 'magical wish gone wrong' idea, but Lucid did it with more finesse and subtlety than most writers."

> \- Gilbert Stack, owner of The Imaginary Realms of Gilbert Stack blog

"There's a creeping paranormal here amongst the normal that tingles those hairs on the back of your neck."
- Geoff Nelder, award-winning author of the Aria trilogy

PART ONE: AWOKEN

August 2012

Mist swirled around where an injured woman lay. The blood flowing from her nose and mouth mingled with her long, silky black hair. Beams from her headlights, and those of another car, lit up the night sky. The running of the other car's engine drowned out the sound of crickets.

After being hit, taking each breath became harder. She had been standing beside her own vehicle when the other driver ploughed into her. She rolled onto the hood and up over the roof, falling back onto the ground with a force like a wrecking ball smashing into her petite body. She immediately felt a few ribs crack and her right leg fracture, and now a great weight rested on her chest, almost as if someone was sitting on it.

A woman was screaming from the other car.

"Oh my God. What did we do? Oh, Lord, there's a girl ... over there. I think we—"

"I ... ca—can't ... die," the injured woman said, her words slurring. "I ... got ... a ... child …" The darkness of unconsciousness crept in from both sides of her vision. Keeping her eyes open was becoming even more of a chore: her lids grew heavier with each passing second, almost as heavy as the increasing weight on her upper body.

Love you, Anna, was the last thought she had before slipping away.

***

Present Day—Deep in the bowels of Hell

Harrowing cries surrounded Malik, along with rivers of fire snaking their way down pre-determined paths. Corrupt politicians were impaled on poles rammed up through their anuses and emerging out their skulls. Horned, winged demons stuffed the politicians' mouths with large fistfuls of dollar bills, and the souls' shouts of agonizing pain added to the already unbearable din of pleas for mercy swirling around Hell.

Bruised and wounded from the lashings he'd received, Malik shuffled along, both his feet and hands shackled. On either side of him stood tall, hulking, oil-black-skinned guards wearing Spartan leather skirts and swords sheathed in brown scabbards. They were fearsome creatures, a sort of wolf and gargoyle hybrid. Malik had the same form but with a thinner frame. They shoved him while continuing on. Heat from the rivers made Malik sweat profusely.

As the bound demon gazed at the wooden bridge that had to be crossed, he moaned, knowing that there were at least another twenty minutes of agony before they reached Satan's throne.

To Malik's far left was a high, ragged cliff. Many mortals were being prodded by the guards' spears, made to jump off into lakes of fire. Their skeletons floated past him, pieces of flesh still clinging to some of the skulls.

Hopefully that won't be me being thrown off the cliff, he thought, each step causing further pain.

Soon they arrived. One guard placed a large hand on Malik's shoulder, forcing him to kneel.

On his throne of bones, Satan sat staring down at him.

Malik dared not look up—not only out of respect and shame, but also due to Satan's hideous appearance. The fallen angel was twelve feet tall, with red-raw skin and a horn looming large on either side of his head. His flaming yellow eyes could penetrate deep into the most hardened soul.

"We meet once more, Malik," Satan boomed.

"Ye—Yes, my lord." Malik's eyes stayed focused on the ground. It pulsed like a human heart.

"You failed me, *again*. That human was supposed to kill those children, and you *failed*!"

"Everything was going well, my lord, until ..." Malik shuddered at the thought of saying Jesus' name. "He intervened."

"Excuses. That's all I hear lately: excuses." Satan banged his humongous fist on the armrest. "There was a time when you were the greatest soldier I had. Convincing Nero to burn Rome—that was a masterpiece. But now, you can barely convince a man to kill a few brats. Oh, how the mighty have fallen."

Satan clicked his fingers. A servant girl with leaches crawling all over her dirty blonde hair, brought him a tray on which stood a silver goblet filled with blood. A section of a human brain bobbed on top of the dark liquid. Satan took a swig, casting those fearsome yellow eyes back to Malik.

"If you just—" Malik began.

"SILENCE!" The King of Hell barked, his roar like thunder. He swirled his drink while pondering Malik's fate. "Mercy isn't usually my forte, but I will give you one last chance. A dead woman's remains have been disturbed and now she's in Limbo. I want you to convince her to get revenge, to kill those who killed her."

"Yes, my lord."

"The humans responsible for her demise are parents to a friend of Jared Duval. He took down two of my best warriors, so I want to make him suffer." Satan gave a carnivorous smile. "I'm allowing you to be ... creative."

"Will I eliminate him, my lord?"

"No. Unfortunately, he's protected by the ... Nazarene. Jared can be hurt but not killed. Watching his friend die will suffice for now."

"I won't let you down."

"See that you don't."

Satan nodded to one of the guards, who stepped forward, unlocking Malik's shackles that were on his dark, leathery skin. Malik sighed with relief, massaging his wrists.

"Go now, before I change my mind," Satan ordered.

Malik rose to leave, but stopped as the king continued: "Failure will see you suffer a punishment so much worse than lashings."

Malik swallowed hard before walking away.

***

When the woman opened her eyes again, she found herself standing in a long, smoky room with black walls. The place stretched out as far as her eyes could see. Victorian-style tilley lanterns hung on both sides, providing meagre light.

Where am I?

"Hello? Is anyone here?" she called out.

Only the echoing of her own words answered.

"Am I in Hell?"

Once more, only her voice, reverberating around the large room.

From some distance behind her, she suddenly heard echoey footsteps. As the figure approached, she discerned the silhouette of a tall man in what appeared to be a navy, pin-striped suit. His face was shadowed by the smoke that was around them.

"Hello?" the woman shouted.

"No need to holler, dear. I can hear you quite well. Don't fret— Malik is here. That's my name; and, from now on, I'll call you Peaches."

The mysterious stranger answered in a calm, self-assured tone as he stepped into the light. His complexion was tanned, and his ginger hair was combed to one side. She noticed a pink handker-chief, folded and sitting in the right breast pocket of his suit.

"My name isn't Peaches," she said. "It's—"

"I know what it is, but that's from a former life," Malik cut in. "I like 'Peaches'. It suits you."

It really doesn't. Wait ... Is this guy the Devil?

"Oh, no," Malik said. "That, I'm not."

Peaches frowned in embarrassment while staring at her feet.

Great, so he can read my thoughts in ... wherever we are.

"Yes, I can ... and don't worry, you'll get used to this after a while."

"Where are we?" Peaches asked.

"Isn't it obvious? We're in Limbo—a kind of halfway place be-tween Heaven and Hell."

"Okay. Then how do I get to Heaven? Can you help me get there?"

Malik put a hand on her right arm. "I'm afraid that won't be happening anytime soon."

Peaches' face became a mask of worry. "But what can you do to help me? Are you an angel?"

"Something like that, yes. What happened to you was a travesty. An injustice. I'm here to make it right." Malik took out a long cigar from inside his jacket. "Do you mind?"

Peaches shook her head.

Malik snipped off the end with a cutter pulled from another pocket, and the cigar's tail end glowed a volcanic orange. He puffed some blue smoke before continuing: "I can take you back home and make those people pay for what they did."

"Wait, won't that stop me from getting into Heaven?"

"Darling, you're not going anywhere for a long while. Time doesn't really exist over here; but if it did, then you'd be in this place for one hundred Earth years. A long time alone, I'm sure you'll agree."

"One hundred years?" Peaches repeated, her eyes beginning to well up with tears.

"That's what I said. Of course, I could shorten that stay or make it more ... tolerable by helping you get justice."

Peaches folded her arms, raising her head and jutting her chin forward. "What's the catch?"

Malik took another drag of his cigar, exhaling more smoke. "No catch. I'm the Angel of Justice ... or in this case, vengeance. I presume you do want to make sure your murderers get what they deserve?"

They did take everything from me. They ripped me away from my baby girl. But can I really trust this guy ... angel ... whatever he is?

"The answer is yes, dear," Malik said.

Damn, I forgot he can read my mind.

"Sorry," said Peaches. "It's just ... This is all so ..."

"Overwhelming? I understand; but this is a one-time offer. Do you want to spend the next hundred years here alone, or go back home and get revenge?"

"I'll never be able to speak to Anna on the phone again, or see her on the weekends," Peaches growled. "Because of *them*."

11

"They did leave you to die like a dog and then hid their dirty deed afterwards. Those heartless mortals didn't give you a second thought."

He's right. I died needlessly, and they get to live. Screw them!

"Let's make them pay," she said.

Malik gave her a wide, ravenous smile, squashing the cigar with his brown leather shoe.

"Music to my ears."

He tucked one hand behind his back; and, like the gentlemen she'd read about in her mother's old Jane Austen books, he offered her the other, as if they were about to dance.

"Shall we, my dear?"

Peaches took Malik's hand. "Yes, let's. How do we go about doing this?"

"First, we'll leave here."

Malik clicked his fingers. A door of pure white light wavered to their right. She could see blue skies. Below them was Hopps Town's main street bustling with cars and people.

"I'll explain as we go through there," Malik said. "Come. Let's have some fun."

Peaches smiled as they walked hand-in-hand towards the luminous portal.

I'm coming for you both, she thought as they stepped through.

***

Present Day—Hopps Town

Jessica picked up the phone and dialed Jared's number. It rang four times before he answered.

"Hel ... Hello?" a groggy Jared said. "Jess? Do you know what time it is?"

"Yeah. I'm sorry, but something crazy just happened."

"What?" Jared sat up, more alert. She had his attention.

"I had a weird dream and got up to go to the bathroom. When I came back, there was a knife in my pillow."

"Whoa. A knife?"

"Uh-huh. And in the dream, I got a warning. I think something's coming after my mom."

Jared yawned and then cleared his throat. "Wait a second. Hold up. Just so we're straight: you had this dream, went to the bathroom, and then you found a knife stuck in your pillow?"

"Yup."

"This is obviously a ghost or something. Look, can we talk about this in the morning—say, 10 a.m. at Jackie's?"

"Okay," Jess said. "Sorry for waking you."

"Don't sweat it. You did the right thing," Jared reassured her. "In the meantime, I'm gonna text you a prayer to say, 'kay?

"All right. See you then."

Just as Jessica was about to hang up, he said, "Oh, and Jess. You still there?"

"Yeah."

"Bring the knife. I'll explain tomorrow."

"Got it."

Two minutes after she'd hung up, Jessica's phone pinged. She opened the message: a picture of the Archangel Michael in a Roman centurion uniform holding a bronze shield and sword, the tip of the blade glinting in the sunlight. Beside him was the famous Archangel Michael Protection Prayer in a beautiful, handwriting-style font. Jessica recited it, asking for Bertha, her mother, to be protected too.

The next morning, Jessica sat two seats down from the diner door. She cut the hot Danish pastry in half, buttered it, and took a bite.

"Mmm." The butter melted into the layers of dough, just the way she liked it.

While eating, she noticed that Jackie had put up a few more black and white pictures of baseball legends on shelves overhead. The color of their menus had been changed from white to a pale green.

The bell over the door dinged, making Jessica look up. Jared entered and walked toward her.

"Hey, Jess," he said. "'Sup?"

"Well, I've been better."

"Yeah, dumb question. My bad."

A waitress came over with a pen and notepad in her hand.

"Can I get you something, sir?" she asked Jared.

"Uh, a strawberry milkshake to go, please."

"Anything to eat?"

"Nah. I'm good, thanks."

"One strawberry milkshake coming up."

Jared waited until she was gone, then leaned slightly over the table. "So, guess you didn't get much sleep last night, huh?"

"No," Jessica confirmed. "It was totally crazy."

"What was your dream about?"

Jessica took another bite of the Danish and sipped some of her mocha latte. "I was getting on a bus to go back to college. Next thing, I'm standing in the hallway of my house. I heard crying in Mom's room; and, when I went in, there was this girl standing there, holding a knife. She said something about Mom 'paying' and she stabbed her. I woke up, and—"

"Went to the bathroom, then saw the same knife in your bed?"

"It was kinda like it, but not the same."

"Well, you know what I meant."

"Yeah, sorry, you're right. That's what happened."

The waitress brought Jared's milkshake. He thanked her.

"So, what do you think this means?" Jessica asked.

"Obviously, some ghost wants revenge on your mom," Jared said. "She must have really pissed off that woman, though. Can you describe her?"

Jessica paused for a moment, trying to recall the woman's appearance. "Um … I think she was, like, in her early twenties. Long black hair, pale. Around my height."

"Did you bring the knife?"

"Yeah, it's in my car. Do you wanna see it?"

"For sure. You can finish your Danish first, though."

"I intend to."

Jessica swallowed the last bite, making sure every last crumb was eaten.

"Now we can go."

The two paid for their orders, then went to sit in Jessica's car, Jared taking the rest of his milkshake with him. From underneath her seat, Jessica pulled out the knife in a Ziplock bag.

"This is it," she said.

"All right." Jared nodded. "I'm gonna see if I can pick up anything."

He removed it from the bag and exhaled a long sigh, closing his eyes. Despite focusing hard, nothing came to him.

"Can't get anything from this. Let me try again."

Jared felt the object with his right hand and meditated. Slowly, an image of two cars stopped at the side of a road began to form in his mind.

Jared arched his neck back as if hit by an invisible hand, now caught in the full throes of a vision.

Everything became clear. Every detail was enhanced: the smell of smoke coming from the vehicles' exhaust pipes, the dazzling beams from the headlights. There, lying bruised and bloody, was a young woman gasping to take a breath.

"I'm seeing two cars and a girl," he got out. "She's dying."

"What does she look like? Is she the one I saw?"

"Don't know. Let me take a closer look."

In the vision, Jared walked closer to the woman and knelt down on one knee.

"She kind of matches the description you gave me. She's in a lot of pain."

Jared wanted to do something to alleviate her agony, but knew that he couldn't. From the other car, he heard another woman yelling. He couldn't make out her words over the loud engine.

"There's a woman shouting," he told Jessica. "Can't understand what she's sayin' … Whoa!"

"What are you seeing?" Jessica asked.

"Looks like whoever hit this girl is stuffing her in their trunk."

"Can you see who's doing it?"

15

"It's a man, but he's kind of like a shadow. It's late at night, and her headlights are out now. Can't see him fully."

Jared suddenly became rigid. A presence of some sort was near him, almost as if it was creeping up on him.

"There's someone else here."

"Who?"

"Don't—"

"They just discarded me like a dead dog," a female voice said in Jared's mind.

Jared looked around in the darkness of the vision, but he couldn't see anyone.

"Who are you?" he asked.

"Someone who wants justice. I'm gonna get it, too."

"How?"

"You'll see."

"Jared? *Hello?* Answer me!" Jessica barked.

Jared threw his head back again, snapping out of the vision.

"All right, all right," he mumbled to himself. "Chill. Wow, that was intense. Never had something like that happen before."

"Who were you talking to?"

"I think it was that girl you saw."

"What did she say?"

Jared thought about lying to Jessica, not wanting to cause her worry.

Jess's my friend. She deserves the truth.

"Same thing she told you. She's looking for justice."

"Was the lady in the car my mom?" Jessica said, her face awash with fear and mortification.

"Can't really tell. But she's connected somehow. Maybe I can try and talk to this girl."

"Is that wise? I mean, she did stick a knife in my pillow."

"Yeah, but I'll take precautions. I have to do a bit of digging first. You know, see who this woman is."

"Maybe we can do it later. Together? If my mom's in trouble, I need to know."

"All right. I got a few things to do in town. Meet me in an hour

16

at my house." Jared sucked some more milkshake from the straw. "Guess this means you're not going back to college now. What're you going to tell your mom?"

"I'll think of something," Jessica said. "Might stay in a motel for a few days. Don't know. Right now, protecting my mother's more important."

"I dig that." Finishing off the remainder of his drink, Jared belched. "Sorry."

"What about you?" Jessica asked him. "What will your parents say?"

"Hell, if my friend's in danger, there ain't no way I'm going anywhere. You and Adrian mean a lot to me, Jess. Got me through some tough times with Lydia and all. So you can be damn sure I'm gonna do everything I can to help."

"But I don't want you missing out on college because of me. You worked so hard to get there."

"Like I said, you guys are important too. Ma and Pop will have to understand."

Jessica squeezed his left hand in appreciation. "Thanks, Jared."

"It's okay. See you over at my place in an hour."

"Got it."

***

Jessica and Jared sat hunched in front of his laptop. For thirty-five minutes they searched for the woman who died, but found nothing. None of the images popping up on the screen resonated with Jared or resembled who he saw in the vision.

"Don't worry, we'll find out who she is," he said when Jessica frowned.

"I know. It's just ..."

"You're worried about your mom. I get it. But we *will* find out who she is; and when we do, I can talk to her. Maybe find out more."

"Hopefully it'll be sooner rather than later." Jessica stood up, sliding her handbag over the left shoulder. "I gotta go check in on

Mom."

"Did you find a motel to stay in?"

"Yeah, it's only for a couple of days. I have to lay low."

Jared thought about what he was going to say next, choosing his words with care. "You know, Jess, there's gonna come a time where we'll have to tell her about this, so you won't be avoiding her forever."

"I know that. But for now, she can't know I'm here."

"That's cool. I understand. I'll call you later if I find anything."

Jared tossed and turned, not fully able to fall into a deep sleep, waking every few minutes. Frustrated, he sat up, fluffed up his pillows and lay down again. Closing both eyes and taking a deep breath, he eventually drifted off.

He was back at the crash scene from the vision. Lying injured on the road was the dark-haired woman. Blood oozed from her mouth and nose.

Jared held up a hand to shield his eyes from the dazzling beams of the headlights. As he walked closer, the woman turned her head, focusing her attention on him.

"Who are you?" Jared asked.

"I'm not going to make it easy for you to help your friend," she gurgled. "Just know they took everything away from me eight years ago."

"Why are you doing this? Is Jessica's mom involved somehow?"

The woman stayed silent, responding instead with a wide, devilish smile.

Just as he was about to speak, Jared saw *Anna* tattooed on her left wrist. He made a mental note of it.

"Maybe I can help you," he said. "Tell me what you want."

"Told you before." The woman disappeared for a moment; then he felt her cold breath on his neck.

Jared spun around. She stood there, garbed in a white robe.

"I want revenge, and I'm going to get it, too." Her face contorted in anger, and she continued through gritted teeth: "Pass that along to your *friend*."

Behind him, there was a loud boom.

Jared opened his eyes. Sweat ran down his forehead and back.

"Message received loud and clear," he muttered. While the name he saw was still fresh in his mind, Jared opened the drawer in his bedside locker. He pulled out a notepad and pen, scribbling down *Anna*.

She's gotta be connected to that woman somehow. Maybe that's her name.

Later that morning, he phoned Jessica.

"Hey, hope I didn't wake you."

"No, it's okay," she said. "What's up?"

"I had a dream ... well, maybe another vision, of that girl."

"Did she tell you anything else?"

"Not much, except that it happened eight years ago. Oh, and on her wrist there was a tattoo. 'Anna'."

"Huh?"

"'Anna'. That was the tattoo. Think that could be her name?"

"No, girls don't usually tattoo their own names on themselves. It could be a daughter or a sister or something."

"Didn't think of that. Guess you took some detective tips from Adrian, huh?" Jared joked. Jessica laughed, but he could sense both sadness and dread in it.

"There was one other thing she said. She wants revenge."

"Okay. She was obviously killed when that car hit her, but maybe she was wronged somehow, too ... I don't know. But we do know this happened eight years ago, right?"

"Uh-huh."

"So now we can do a new search, using 'Anna', too."

"Cool. Jackie's in two hours?"

"You read my mind. This time breakfast's on me," Jessica said.

"Can you afford that, though?"

"Jared, just take the offer while it lasts."

"All right. Cool. See you then."

***

Jessica and Jared sat scouring Google on their phones. Two empty plates were before them, their cups half filled. Jared had a mocha latte and Jessica an Americano. A white napkin stained with brown blotches from Jared wiping his mouth, was beside the mocha. He tried "missing persons 2012", while Jessica punched in "car accidents in Hopps Town 2012". Neither search proved fruitful.

"Dang. I'm seeing nothing here," Jared admitted.

"Me neither," Jessica replied.

"Maybe we should try something else."

"Sure."

Jared typed in "Anna daughter 2012". The first few pages of results revealed nothing. As he scrolled halfway down page four, an image of a young woman in her twenties grabbed his attention. He clicked on it and immediately felt a cold chill run through his body.

"I found her."

"You did? Can I see?" Jessica's voice bubbled with anticipation.

Jared handed over his phone.

Jessica's eyes widened in shock and her face turned a shade whiter. "That's ... her. She's the one I saw."

"Her name is Tabitha Logan. It says in that article she went missing in 2012. She has a daughter named Anna."

"Okay. I guess it's something to go on, right?"

"Yeah. But like you said, we've gotta be careful. She is *really* angry at your mom. If I'm gonna reach out to her, I've gotta do it somewhere safe."

"Like where?"

Jared thought about it for a minute before answering. "I think in the forest near the park. It's away from people."

"Are you going to do it alone?"

"It might be safer that way. She could attack you if you came along." Jared slid the phone into his pocket.

"When are you gonna do it?"

"Probably this evening. I need to get a few things first for the ritual." Jared drank the remainder of his mocha. "Gotta bounce. I'll text when it's done."

"All right. Just be careful."

***

Jared pulled into his parents' driveway. The store he'd gone to had closed early, and wouldn't open again until tomorrow.

"Damn!" he shouted, banging the steering wheel in frustration. *Just hope Jess and her mom will be okay for another night.*

When he opened the front door, Maria Duval's humming could be heard coming from the kitchen, accompanied by the enticing aromas of spicy food. He'd forgotten that she'd promised to make her special curry tonight.

"Hey Ma," he said quickly. "Just gonna do some studying in my room."

Maria stopped chopping the chilies and peppers.

"Jared, honey, can we have a quick chat?"

Jared groaned, knowing instinctively where this 'quick chat' was about to go. "Look, I don't really wanna do this today, all right?"

"No, it's not *all right*. I'm concerned about you, baby. You're missing a week of college. By the time you get back, you could be behind."

"Don't sweat it, Ma. My friend is emailing me notes and the assignments we have to do. I'm doing those while I'm finishing this case."

"Jared, sit down." When he didn't, Maria gave him a pleading look, and he obliged.

"I get that you're embracing your role ... gift ... whatever you want to call it God gave you," she said, taking a seat opposite him. "And don't get me wrong: I'm proud of you. But you can't keep putting people before your education, son."

"I know, and I'm not, but Jess isn't just another person. She's my friend. More than that—she was there and stuck up for me when I first came out. Adrian and her got me through some really

21

tough times. If I have to miss a week or two of college, so be it."

Maria took a deep breath. Jared could see that she was trying to remain calm. "Jared, the opportunity to go to college only comes around once. Believe me, you don't wanna leave it until you're forty. It might be hard now, but it's even harder at that age. I should know."

"You're worried about me, and that's cool. I get that. But there are things going on that aren't everyday problems, Ma. Jess and her mom are in danger."

Maria's brow furrowed. Her concerned expression grew even grimmer. "Out of curiosity, on a scale of one to ten, how dangerous is ... whatever it is you're facing?"

Jared got up, pushing in his chair. "Not answering that. We've been over this before. This is my life now, whether I like it or not. This is what God put me here to do."

"Well excuse me for being concerned, but you're my son, Jared! It's my job to worry about you. I don't like you going up against these ... *things*."

"That's what I'm here to do. And I say this with love, Ma, but get used to it."

"That's the problem, I can't!" Maria banged her hands on the table, all her composure completely lost. "Do you know what it feels like for me, as your mother, to not be able to protect you while you're out there bustin' ghosts? Do you know how useless I feel for not being able to protect you?"

"I'm not a baby anymore. Aunt Maybelle taught me well. And if I'm ever in a jam, she said she'd help me."

"She ain't gonna be around forever too. What are you gonna do then?"

"Solve it on my own." Jared rubbed his own forehead, feeling a dull, pulsating throb. "I can't do this now. I'm going to my room."

"Speaking of Aunt Maybelle, you talk to her recently?"

"No. Why? Is she all right?"

"Give her a call. She'll tell you herself."

***

Jared's phone rang twice before Aunt Maybelle answered.

"Was wondering when you'd call," she said.

Jared closed his bedroom door. "Mom told me to. What's up?"

"My leg, that's what."

"Huh?"

"I'm in hospital. Broke my ankle."

"You did what?" Jared said, his voice raised in exasperation. "How the *hell* did that happen?"

"Went into a grocery store two days ago. The idiot owner never put up a wet floor sign. Let's just say wet floors and high heels don't make a great combination. Next thing I know, I'm lying on my ass and my right ankle is broke. Now I'm laid up here for a week or two."

"Aw, sorry to hear that. How you gonna cope when you get out?"

"Your dad's coming up for a few weeks to help. The military gave him two weeks' leave. He told me last night."

"Wish I could be there to lend a hand too."

"Just focus on college."

"Don't you start. Already had that chat with Ma."

"Listen to her. She's right."

Jared was silent for a moment. He struggled with whether or not to ask a question.

"Got something on your mind? Maybe a question for old Aunt Belle?"

"Still doing the Jedi mind-reading tricks, huh?"

They shared a brief laugh, and then he told her about Tabitha Logan.

"Ooh ... That sounds like a vengeful spirit, like Caleb Hammerson. Those dudes can be tricky. And dangerous. Gotta watch your back on this one, J."

"Tell me about it." Jared sighed, not wanting to show too obviously that he wished she was here with him. "Just hope you get better soon."

"I know you're scared, but don't be. You got this. Besides, I

23

can't always be there. It's time to fly the nest. So take that leap, little bird."

"Thanks. I'll call you in a couple of days."

"You better, or I'll get Grandma to pay a visit and kick your butt."

They laughed again, and Jared hung up.

***

Bertha Barlow sat in her office, scowling as she glared at the computer monitor. Today had not been smooth sailing. Two deliveries didn't arrive, and three employees phoned in sick with Covid. Now she had to do an extra shift to make up for the lack of manpower.

After typing the last few figures into an Excel spreadsheet, Bertha tried clicking on the floppy disc icon, but it wouldn't save. She shuffled the mouse. The cursor stayed still.

"No, no, don't do this to me, please." Bertha pressed Control, Alt and Delete. Again, nothing happened.

"Crap!" she grumbled. "Well, why not? Everything else has gone sideways today."

Bertha got up and took a packet of cigarettes from her green jacket hanging on the office door.

"Gotta get some fresh air."

While she stood outside smoking, in her peripheral vision she saw a dark-haired girl. Bertha turned her head.

The figure was gone.

"Guess I was seeing things." She shook her head, dismissing it, and finished the cigarette.

A few minutes later, Bertha went to wash her hands in the ladies' room. As she dried them under the heater, the lights dimmed and flickered.

"Another power surge?"

The heater cut out, and Bertha dabbed at her hands with toilet paper before heading to the door. She pulled the handle, but it wouldn't budge. Two more tugs brought her no luck.

"All right, guys. Enough with the jokes. Open up."

She waited for a few moments for the door to open, or to hear it being unlocked from outside.

Nothing.

"This isn't funny anymore," Bertha yelled, pounding on the wood in frustration. "Unlock the damn door!"

"What's wrong, boss?" A man's voice said from the other side. It was Norman, a tall, skinny twenty-something who always wore purple-rimmed spectacles.

"Did you lock this door?" Bertha demanded.

"No."

"Then why can't I—" Bertha was interrupted by the lights going out. She stood in darkness. "Looks like we got a power cut."

"What do you mean? The lights are on out here."

"Then how—" Once more she was stopped, this time by a toilet flushing. "Is anyone in here? Hello?"

A door creaked, but Bertha couldn't see if anyone had come out of the cubicle next to the one she'd used.

"Stacey, is that you?" she asked. Stacey was the only other female member of staff on shift today.

The slow methodical *kop, kop, kop* of high heels walking towards her sent Bertha's heart racing.

"Stacey, quit playing around!" Bertha yelled.

"Boss, are you okay?" asked Norman. "Stacey's out here."

"Norman, get the keys. Quick!" Bertha twisted the handle feverishly and shook the door as the footsteps drew closer. "Open, damn it."

The sound of something hitting glass made Bertha jump. The lights came on.

There, less than three feet away from her, was the imprint of a fist in the corner of a shattered mirror.

"How in God's name ...?" Bertha was left speechless as she backed away.

She jumped again as the main door opened a crack. Craning her neck, Bertha couldn't see anyone outside. She swallowed, coming to the realization that it had opened by itself.

"What's going on here?" Bertha muttered. Without wasting any time, she ran out of the bathroom.

***

Jared rubbed his eyes; they were heavy from tiredness. He had been studying for the last three hours, and also read over the notes Maybelle gave him after they defeated Caleb Hammerson's ghost and the demon who assisted him. Part of him knew that tomorrow could bring anything his way, while he was performing the ritual. But as Aunt Maybelle had told him many times: "Don't let fear stand in the way of doing your job. Trust in Jesus."

"Let's just hope you're right, Aunt Belle," Jared said while closing his textbook.

Jared's phone vibrated, and he saw Jessica's name on the screen.

"Yo, Jess, what's up?"

"So, did you do the ritual?" she asked.

"Nah, the store closed early. I'll get what I need in the morning and I'll do it then. Don't worry, it'll be done."

"Great. Call me first thing when you're finished, okay?"

"Don't worry. I will."

Jessica sighed and sniffled. "Sorry for annoying you. I'm just ..." Her voice trembled and he heard a gasp.

"Worried? Hey, you don't have to tell me. Been there and done that. We'll sort this. Promise."

"Thanks. Better let you go and get some sleep. Got a busy day tomorrow."

"It'll be fine, Jess. Don't sweat it. Goodnight."

"Night."

Jared hung up. Lying wasn't something he liked doing, but it was the only way to calm Jessica's nerves. There was no telling what could happen, but he hoped that it would be a step towards saving Bertha.

Jared got dressed for bed. As he was changing, the light bulb in his lamp blew out. He switched it on and off, but the light didn't come back on.

"Dang," Jared grumbled. As he placed a hand on the doorknob, a cool breeze blew across his neck. Spinning around, he glanced at the window. It was closed.

Guess I got company.

"Who's there? Show yourself." Jared's eyes scanned every corner of the room as he went to get the crucifix from his locker. "In Jesus' name, I command you to show yourself."

The room began to grow cold. Hairs on his arms stood on end; a frosty chill circled his feet.

"Oh no," Jared mumbled.

Raising the crucifix like a sword, Jared began reciting a protection prayer. "Saint Michael the Archangel, defend us in battle. Be our—"

A freezing hand covering his mouth interrupted him.

"Shh ..." Tabitha whispered into his left ear. "Want to know more about me? Fine. Let me show you."

Her hand moved to his eyes, and Jared felt himself being sucked into a void, a dark tunnel, not knowing where it would lead him.

He hoped it wouldn't be to his doom.

PART TWO: THE LIFE OF TABITHA LOGAN

Jared's screams were muffled as he hurtled towards a blinding white light. It felt like being sucked into a vacuum, an invisible magnetic force pulling him in. He landed on his feet, suddenly finding himself standing in a pitch-black room with mist swirling around his ankles.

Jared turned around as someone approached. A little spotlight shone, and Tabitha came into view.

"Where are we? What am I doing here?" Jared asked.

"You wanted to know about me, so here we are." Tabitha pointed to one of the walls.

A white screen appeared, filling with the image of a young girl, alone in a kitchen. She sat at a small, circular table with an empty plate in front of her. Her arms were folded, and there was a large frown on her face. The girl's eyes were red from crying.

"Is that you?" Jared asked.

Tabitha spoke to him telepathically.

"I never had it easy growing up. My mama always found it hard to make ends meet. Daddy died in a drive-by shooting when I was born. Some days I went hungry after coming home from school. Mama was never around, always trying to find work."

The scene switched to an older Tabitha working in a grocery store and, later, flipping burgers in a fast-food joint.

"At sixteen, I left school, and had to get two jobs just so we could afford to eat and pay the rent," she explained. "Hated every minute of it. While everyone else was out enjoying themselves, I was slaving away—until eleven, some nights. I did this for two years, crying myself to sleep when I came home. But everything changed when I met Ron."

Tabitha now sat in a diner, across from a young man who had scruffy brown hair, an unkempt beard, sparkling blue eyes and a roguish smile. Jared could see why she'd been so attracted to him. He liked the "bad boy" type, too; but even from the image on the screen, he could sense that Ron wasn't a good person.

Teenage Tabitha stared into Ron's eyes: lovestruck and in awe of him, hanging on his every word.

"Ron was three years older," Tabitha continued in Jared's

29

mind. "We met at a nightclub. It was love at first sight. I knew he was the one. He said he'd take care of me, always buying nice things, showing me the kind of affection no-one else did. For the first time in my life, other girls were jealous of me—especially of my fancy jewelry. Ron said he worked in construction, but I could never understand how he afforded all that stuff on a small salary."

Jared watched as the kitchen reappeared, showing eighteen-year-old Tabitha arguing with her mother, Imelda. The older woman had long, sandy hair tied up in a ponytail. There were dark circles around her eyes, and an aura of weariness seemed to envelope her.

"Mama warned me about Ron, saying he was no good. I thought we were gonna be together forever. Guess I should've listened to her …" The Tabitha in the spotlight shook her head. "Anyway, me and Ron shacked up together, and soon we had a young 'un of our own."

The image faded, and another scene wavered into view, this time of a hospital room. Tabitha held a newborn baby in her arms, while Ron and her mother stood by her side crying tears of joy.

"We named her Anna, after my grandma. Things were good between us for a while. Ron was a doting dad, buying Anna new clothes and toys. Her room was full of teddy bears. Should've known the good times wouldn't last."

An alarm blared, making Jared jump. Ron and two other men, all wearing ski masks, ran out of a jewelry store with duffle bags slung over their shoulders. Each of them held sawn-off shotguns. They dashed to a car parked just a few feet away. After throwing the bags into the trunk, they drove off.

"I didn't know what Ron was up to. Never figured he robbed stores for a livin'," Tabitha snarled. "The idiot thought he got away with this one, too, but he wasn't so smart. Police caught the side of his face on CCTV when he took off his mask. When they found out who he was, they came a-lookin'. Ron got wind of the situation from a buddy of his, and he left me high and dry with Anna before they came to our house. The cops had a hard time believing me when I said I didn't know anything about his crimes, but they eventually let me go. It's not surprising that I never heard from him again."

"What happened then?" Jared asked out loud.

"I had no choice but to move back in with my mom," Tabitha replied. "Couldn't afford the rent, so for the next four years I went from job to job, trying to earn enough for Anna and me to get a place of our own. There were times I wished that I could stay with a good boss and people who I could call friends. Never thought that would happen, until one day ..."

With her head down and shoulders slouched, a dejected Tabitha walked by Belvedere's Bookstore. On the window was a flyer with the words *Staff Wanted. Apply instore.*

Tabitha headed inside. There was an old-world charm to this place, with its teak bookshelves containing worn first editions of modern classics like *To Kill a Mockingbird, Catcher in the Rye* and *The Hobbit*. To the right, accentuating the store's quirky style, stood an antique desk, with an old typewriter—Jared guessed it was from the 1940s or 50s. A vintage lamp with an emerald-green shade stood beside it.

Tabitha glanced around for the owner.

"Hello?" she called out. When there was no response, she tried again.

"Hello? Is anyone here?"

"Yes, be with you in a minute," a female voice called out from the back. A few seconds later, a short, elderly lady with bobbed gray hair and a dark-green uniform stepped out from behind a row of gardening books. The gold name badge pinned to her sweater read *Dorothy.*

"How can I help you?" Dorothy spoke with a certain elegance.

"I was just passing by and I saw the notice on your window. Are you still looking for staff?"

"Yes, we are. Do you have a résumé?"

"Uh ... Sure." Tabitha reached inside the manila envelope she was carrying and handed a copy to Dorothy.

She glanced over it, an eyebrow arching. "Wow, I see you've worked in a lot of places. None for more than a year, though. How come?"

"They either closed down or that job wasn't right for me."

"And what makes you think this place is 'right' for you?"

"I've never worked in a book store before, and I'd like to give it a try."

"So you like trying new things, huh?"

"Yes, ma'am, I do."

"Oh, please call me Dorothy. Ma'am makes me feel old."

Dorothy took another look at the résumé and handed it back to Tabitha.

"Tell you what," Dorothy said, "I'll give you a two-day trial run. How does that sound?"

"Thank you! That would be amazing."

Dorothy showed Tabitha around, pointing out where books in certain genres were stocked and how the cash register worked.

"Everything ran smoothly the first day," Tabitha went on in Jared's mind. "Dorothy even treated me to lunch. Second day though, I messed up with the money, giving someone a bit more change than I should've. I kept quiet, hoping she wouldn't notice. Maybe I hoped for too much."

On the screen, Tabitha was stacking the last few Tom Clancy novels in the thriller and espionage section when she noticed, through the back office's open door, Dorothy scrutinizing the day's receipts. Her eyes were narrowed, and she was scratching her head in confusion. She punched some numbers into a calculator, again shaking her head.

"Tabitha, dear, can you come in here, please?" she called.

Tabitha swallowed hard and began sweating. She crossed the short distance to the office, mentally bracing herself for a dressing-down.

"Yes, Dorothy?" she said, feigning ignorance.

"Something doesn't add up here. We're ten dollars out. Can you explain that?"

"Well, I didn't take anything, if that's what you mean."

"Then where did it go?"

"Maybe I gave too much change to some customer?"

"It's possible ..." Dorothy sat back in her chair, putting down the receipts and calculator. "You know, dear, I'm taking a risk giving you a trial run, what with your employment history." She clucked her tongue, her gaze switching back to Tabitha from the computer screen. "If this happens again, you will be fired. Understand?"

"Yes," Tabitha said. "Thanks for giving me another chance."

"Go before I change my mind. You've another hour on your shift."

Tabitha walked away briskly, breathing a sigh of relief.

She stocked more shelves, and put up posters promoting a book signing that was to be held in a week's time, until Dorothy called her back.

"Money slip-up aside, I think you did good work," she said. "So I'm going to give you another two-day trial, and I'll let you know then."

"Thanks, Dorothy. I really appreciate it. See you tomorrow."

Tabitha picked up her coat and bag, walking out of the store with a broad smile.

"The next two days went well," Tabitha elaborated, "and I hoped she'd hire me. A week later, she did. It meant so much to me to be given a chance. Now I was back working again, and I could really focus on finding somewhere for myself and Anna.

"Two months go by, and, for the first time in a long while, I felt like I was somewhere I belonged. Dorothy was like a second mother, buying me doughnuts, giving advice on personal matters, and she even bought Anna some clothes. My mama was kind of jealous, but I was just glad to have a friend like her. In my third month there, a woman came in and gave me a warning I should've listened to."

As Tabitha put some heavy tomes back on their assigned shelves, a woman wearing purple pants and a black shawl draped around her shoulders caught her attention. There was something about this lady in her early forties, browsing through New Age books, that drew Tabitha in.

The customer brought a title by Louise Hay to the checkout

counter.

Tabitha scanned it. "That's seven dollars and ten cents, please."

The lady pulled out a ten dollar bill. "I don't have anything smaller."

"That's fine."

Jared noticed that the mystery woman's gaze never left Tabitha as she dropped the change into her palm.

"Do you mind if I ask you a question?" the customer asked.

"Not at all."

"Would you mind if I read your palm? Do you believe in palm readings?"

Tabitha stared back in silence for a moment, words eluding her.

"Um .. .I don't know. If you're selling it, then no, sorry."

"I'm not going to charge anything."

The woman gently held Tabitha's hand. Her eyes roved over every line crisscrossing Tabitha's palm—then her lips turned down.

"Do be careful of those corners," she cautioned. "You just never know what comes around them. Don't stay there for long."

"Wait ... What does that mean?"

"You'll know when it happens. Just heed my words, love. Don't hang around corners too long. Good day to you."

Nodding her head in farewell, the fortune-teller walked out.

"I didn't know what she meant at the time but boy, was she right!" Tabitha fumed.

"Are you talking about the accident?" Jared asked.

"You'll see. Over the next few months, I noticed Dorothy was at the store less and less. She got paler, and a little thinner. I hoped and prayed there was nothing serious wrong with her. Guess my prayers fell on deaf ears.

"One day, she told me we'd have a chat later in her office. I thought I was about to lose my job. But what she had to tell me was much worse."

Tabitha flipped the *open* sign to *closed*. As she began sweeping the floor, Dorothy called out to her.

"Tabbie, can you come here, please?"

It was the moment she dreaded. With her heart pounding, Tabitha leaned the broom against the wall and went into the office.

"Yes, Dorothy?"

"Sit down."

Tabitha remained standing. "Did I do something wrong? Am I being fired?"

Dorothy chuckled while replying, "God, no. You did nothing wrong, dear." Pointing to the only other seat, she said in a soft, sweet voice, "You're not being fired. Don't worry. Please sit."

With pursed lips and eyebrows drawn together in concern, Tabitha sat. "What is it?"

"As you may have noticed, I'm not here as often as I was."

"Yeah, I saw that, but I didn't want to say anything. Is there ...?" Tabitha found it hard to finish that sentence, trying with all her might to fight back the welling tears.

"That's because I've not been feeling well for a while," Dorothy confirmed. "Turns out ... I have lung cancer."

Tabitha gasped, raising a hand to her mouth. She lost her battle to restrain her emotions, tears blurring her vision before rolling down her cheeks. Her lips began to tremble. "Is it ...?"

"Terminal? No, they caught it in time. But I will have to undergo some chemotherapy, which means I'm going to be gone a lot more."

"Does this mean the store's closing down?"

"No! It's has been in my family for the last fifty years. While I'm gone, I'm going to need someone to run it. So I'm making you the manager."

Tabitha sat in dumbfounded silence.

"God, Dorothy, I don't know what to say," she finally got out.

"I think 'thank you' would be a start," Dorothy replied, with her trademark sarcastic wit. "Seriously, Tabbie, you've earned it. I couldn't imagine a better person running this place in my absence."

"Oh my gosh. Thank you for believing in me! But I don't know if I can run it on my own."

"I don't expect you to. That's why we're going to be holding interviews. We're hiring another person."

"Okay. Thank you so much!"

Tabitha hugged Dorothy, both out of gratitude and to console her for the difficulties she was about to face.

"That was one of the best and saddest moments of my life. Someone actually saw something in me, thought I was worth putting in charge; but there was a chance I'd lose a good friend." Tabitha paused, long enough for Jared to realize just how deeply these events had affected her. "When I told mama about my promotion, she was delighted.

"Over the next few weeks, I spent more evenings in the office with Dorothy while she showed me the ropes: how to balance the books, how to order more stock, and other things a boss does. But she was missing more and more; and, eventually, she couldn't come in at all. I so wanted to see her, in the hospital or at her house, but Dorothy didn't want visitors. Part of me felt she didn't like people seeing her without any hair.

"Two months into the treatment, she sent me pictures of her wig. On anyone else it wouldn't have worked, but it did on her.

"The store just wasn't the same without Dorothy. We hired another girl named Theresa. She was perfect and always had the shelves stocked. The customers liked her, too.

"Another four months went by. Then Dorothy phoned with some good news: her treatment had worked. Her cancer had been contained, even shrunk, and she talked about coming back to work, starting out with just a day or two and then building on that over time. I couldn't wait to have her back. She set a date, and I knew we had to do something special."

Acting as a look-out, Theresa stood by the door, keeping a watchful eye on the street. Tabitha prepared a few side tables with some bottles of soda, plastic cups and little bowls of potato chips and mini chocolate bars. A large *Welcome Back* banner hung over the second row of books.

"I sure hope she likes what you did here," an old lady said to Tabitha.

"Me too. I'm sure she will."

"Dorothy's coming!" Theresa announced excitedly.

"Okay, everyone, here we go," Tabitha said.

Theresa rushed to Tabitha's side, and all the customers stood behind them.

Dorothy walked with her head low, searching for the right key. When it clicked in the lock and she looked up, her free hand went up to her mouth. A smile spread across her face while she eyed the banner and crowd standing underneath it.

Tabitha opened the door. Dorothy caught her in an appreciative embrace, squeezing her tightly.

"Oh, thank you," she whispered into Tabitha's ear.

"Let me look at you," Tabitha said, taking a step back. Dorothy had regained some of the weight she lost. Some of the radiant glow she'd had when they first met also returned. "Wow, you look great."

"You did a marvelous job with this place, dear. Well done."

Theresa was next to hug Dorothy. Soon, others welcomed her too, shaking her hand or wrapping her in their arms.

After fifteen minutes of speaking and mingling with the customers, Dorothy filled a cup with soda. Clearing her throat, she tapped the table to get everyone's attention. A hush gradually fell over the crowd.

"I just want to say a few words. For the last six months, I've dreamt about a day like this, being able to come back and do my job. Seeing you all here today has made all my struggles seem worth it. A big thank you to my wonderful staff, Tabitha and Theresa. They kept this place afloat while I was away. Thanks to everyone for coming here over the years. We couldn't have survived without you." Waving a hand over the banner and table full of drinks and snacks, she continued, "And seeing all the trouble you guys went to today has made me realize just how blessed I am." Dorothy fanned her face, her voice breaking. "I'm going to stop now before I cry."

There was a collective "aww" from the crowd before Tabitha hugged Dorothy again. Everyone applauded her speech as she wiped tears from her cheeks with a cream-colored handkerchief.

Pointing once more to the drinks table, she said, "Come on, everyone. Drink up."

"Over the next six months, Dorothy slowly returned to normal," Tabitha went on. "It was great having her in the store again. I missed our chats, and the advice she loved to give. I noticed she spent a lot of time in her office, constantly on the phone. Part of me was scared that the cancer had grown worse and she'd have to take more time off. Any chance I got, I'd pretend to be doing something near her office while she was talking. Once, I overheard that her son purchased a new building and something about moving. I wondered if she'd up sticks and shift her store to somewhere else, leaving me and Theresa without jobs.

"One day, Dorothy called me in for a chat. I was worried that there'd be bad news, but nothing prepared me for what she was about to tell me."

Tabitha sat in the other chair, crossing and uncrossing her arms and ankles, finding it hard to be at ease.

Dorothy placed a hand on Tabitha's leg. "Don't worry, Tabbie, I'm not going to be the bearer of bad news. Quite the opposite, actually."

"Oh yeah?"

"Yes. As luck would have it, he bought a building in a place called Hopps Town. It's about twenty miles from here. Ever hear of it?"

Tabitha shook her head.

"Lovely little place. Anyway, I'm thinking of expanding the business and setting up a store there."

"Oh." Tabitha put a hand to her chest, relieved.

"Wait a minute, did you think I was moving there and leaving you and Theresa behind?"

"Well, I didn't know what to think."

"Tabitha, darling, I wouldn't do that. You kept this place going while I was out sick. I'd never do that to you."

"Thanks. I was so scared that I'd have to start looking for a new job."

"No, not at all! But I am going to tell you something else, and I want you to think it over, all right?"

"O ... kay," Tabitha replied, concerned. Her heart raced a little. Her blue eyes blinked rapidly. A sudden sense of tightness rose around them.

"I can't be in two places at once," Dorothy said, "and the doctors say that constant travel and stress could aggravate the cancer. I'm going to need someone in charge in Hopps Town, and I think you're the right person for the job."

Speechless, Tabitha stared back at Dorothy, her jaw lowered in shock.

"Well ... what are your thoughts on that?"

"I ... don't know what to say. I mean, my family's here."

"I understand, but this is a big opportunity. You got great ideas, and I think you can really make a go of it there." Moving her chair in a little closer, Dorothy cupped Tabitha's hands in her own. "This is a lot to take in, I know, but at least think about it. Will you do that?"

"Uh ... yes, of course."

Later, Tabitha met Imelda at the park. Anna walked between them as they discussed Dorothy's proposal.

"So, you gonna take it?" Imelda asked.

"I don't know what to do," Tabitha admitted.

"If you do go, are you taking Anna with you?"

"Obviously. I'm not gonna just go and leave her behind. You've helped raise her since the start—I couldn't have done it without you, and it wouldn't be fair to either of you to just dump her on her grandma." Tabitha bit her lip. "I feel so bad about what happened with Ron. Ashamed, actually."

"That wasn't entirely your fault, honey. He had me fooled for a while, too."

"But you did warn me about him. Should've listened to you."

Imelda sighed. "That's what love does, makes a person do silly things."

"If I did move to Hopps Town, would you visit?"

"Damn right I would." Bending down to Anna, Imelda said, "Nobody's gonna stop me from seeing my little princess." After kissing her on the cheek, she straightened up again. "There's a lot to mull over, Tabitha, honey. I'd take it, but it's not my choice."

"Yeah. I've got a lotta thinking to do."

Tabitha turned to Jared, a wry smile on her face.

"That night, I didn't sleep much, but Mama was right. This was a once-in-a-lifetime opportunity. This wasn't taking over the store for a couple of months. I'd be running one full-time. So, the next morning, I told Dorothy I'd do it; and I went looking around for a place to rent in Hopps Town that were big enough for two people. They had a great elementary school there for Anna. Dorothy wasn't kidding; it was a lovely little place.

"The new store opened two months later. Dorothy and Mama were there for the celebration, and some photographers came by from local newspapers. Business was slow at first, but things picked up as word spread around town. I even took night classes in marketing once a week. As for Anna, she fit right in with the other kids. The cost of childcare cut into what I was earning, but we had enough.

"When spring rolled around, I got a huge surprise in the mail. The good kind."

Tabitha was rooted to the spot, her eyes widened in surprise, holding a letter in her hand. Jacintha, another staff member, noticed as she walked by.

"What's wrong?" Jacintha asked.

"I can't believe it! We won the Best New Business Award!"

"What?" Jacintha grabbed the paper. She stared for a while, then whistled in amazement. "Wow, this is incredible!"

"I can't believe it," Tabitha repeated. "I gotta tell Dorothy!"

Tabitha rushed to the office. She dialed the number quickly, tapping her left foot in excited anticipation as the phone rang.

"Belvedere Bookstore. Dorothy speaking," said the familiar voice on the other end. "How may I help you?"

"It's Tabbie. You'll never guess what just happened. I got a letter from the local business committee. We were just voted the best new business in Hopps Town!"

"Please don't let this be a joke."

"No, I'm serious!"

"Oh my God, that's fantastic news. We've got to make the most out of this."

"My thoughts exactly. The committee is sending over a few photographers and the mayor to mark the event on the nineteenth. So here's what I was thinking …"

For the next few minutes, Tabitha divulged her ideas about having a twenty-percent-off sale on that day.

"That's great, but make it fifteen," Dorothy suggested. "We want to make a profit, not a loss."

"All right. You're the boss."

"And you are a godsend. Well done, Tabbie. This is a magnificent achievement."

A week later, balloons and fifteen-percent-off stickers were placed throughout the store. A banner hung outside, announcing Hopps Town's Belvedere Bookstore's accomplishment. Imelda came to take care of Anna. She proudly announced to anyone who would listen that Tabitha was her daughter.

Customers started to file in, and even more came when they noticed Dorothy and Tabitha standing outside with the mayor, being photographed. Tabitha and Dorothy held a trophy between them, smiling for the cameras.

That evening, when the store was closed, Dorothy took a beaming Tabitha into the office.

"I have to head back," she said. "Today was a great success. I'm so proud of you, Tabbie." Dorothy hugged her tightly.

"Aw, thanks, Dor." Tabitha's voice broke and she cleared her throat. "Thanks for … believing in me."

Dorothy stood back, holding the young woman's shoulders.

"Why do I still get a feeling of doubt from you? Isn't this award proof you were worth taking on?"

"Yeah … but … I just feel so … overwhelmed and blessed. Up until a year ago, nothing went right for me, and now this all feels like a dream. I don't want it to end."

"Keep up the good work and sky's the limit for you," Dorothy soothed, wiping away Tabitha's tears. "Someday, you might even own your own business."

"D'ya really think that could happen?"

"Of course. Anything is possible with the kind of effort that you put in here. *Believe* in yourself, Tabbie. I do."

They hugged once more, Tabitha closing her eyes for a few seconds, relishing the moment. She opened them again; and, staring up beyond the ceiling, she mouthed, "Thank you."

"That day was the greatest of my life. Finally, people other than Dorothy saw how hard I worked, that I was more than my past. Mama never stopped smiling throughout the opening. We celebrated that night and drank into the small hours. Good thing I didn't have to go into work the next morning.

"Two weeks later, Dorothy gave me the weekend off. I was gonna use that time to go home and spend it with Mama." Tabitha's voice dropped, becoming low and bitter. "But God had other plans."

Tapping the steering wheel, Tabitha kept reminding herself that there was only another half hour to go. Driving by night was something she hated, and breaking down the journey into four thirty-minute slots made it easier to get through. Imelda had already picked up Anna, who'd had a few days off from school due to a nasty stomach bug.

As Tabitha passed a junction, the orange 'check engine' light came on.

"Aw, no. Not now."

The car spluttered, and soon she had to pull over.

"Damn," she cursed. Tabitha turned off the ignition, got out of the car and popped the hood. Waving away the smoke, she took a look.

"What the hell is wrong here?"

After waiting a few minutes for the oil and water caps to cool down, Tabitha checked the fluid levels. There was enough of both.

"What am I going to do now?"

No sooner had she asked herself this than Tabitha's face grew white. The fortune-teller's warning played in her mind: *Just be careful around corners.* That was where she found herself, in the middle of a bend on the road.

I gotta get outta here.

Tabitha unlocked her phone to check her signal. Despite finding none, she stood by her car and tried calling Imelda. The flat busy tone was drowned out by the engine of an approaching car taking the corner too fast.

Before Tabitha could react, it plowed straight into her.

Jared stared at the screen, slack-jawed. Now that he'd seen how she died in such graphic detail, he understood Tabitha's rage.

Tabitha stepped in front of him, patches of her pale face burning angry red to match the fury in her eyes.

"Now you know what it felt like, having everything ripped away from me," she stormed. "Never able to see my Anna again, but they keep on living like nothing happened!"

"Look, Ms. Logan ..." Jared fumbled. "I'm sorry you died that way. It was an accident, though."

"At first. But they didn't even ring a damn ambulance. They just covered their tracks."

"Wait ... what do you mean, 'covered their tracks?'"

"That bitch will have to tell you."

"You mean Jessica's mom?"

Tabitha nodded.

"I can understand why you're angry, but why did you show me this?"

"Because you wanted to know about me. Now you do, and you'll understand why I gotta do what I need to."

Jared swallowed hard, his concern growing for both Bertha and Jessica. "What do you mean by that?"

"You'll see." Tabitha touched his forehead.

Jared gasped as he sat up in bed, drenched with sweat. He checked his bedside clock, which read *04:30*.

"I'll wait three hours to ring Jessica," he said to himself. "I gotta warn her."

He lay down again, knowing that sleeping would be the last thing he'd do.

43

PART THREE: REVENGE

Dawn broke, and Jared's room gradually became brighter as the sun's rays poured in.

Time to ring Jess, he thought. *Just hope she's up.*

A few minutes after switching on his phone, he received a text message from her.

Good luck with the ritual today. Let me know if it works.

Jared replied: *Meet you at Bunker Hill at 9 a.m. Got something I have to tell you.*

Jared stopped his Renault Clio on top of Bunker Hill, wondering how to break the news to Jessica.

She pulled up in her own car soon after. She smiled, waving at him before turning off the engine and climbing into his vehicle.

"Hey," Jessica said.

"Hi."

"So, what is it you want to tell me?"

"Last night, Tabitha paid me a visit. She showed me, like, a video of her life, and how she died—"

"And?" Jessica's forehead was wrinkled in worry.

"She was knocked down by a car."

"Is my mom connected to this?"

Jared stayed silent, afraid to answer.

"Well?" Jessica said, more insistent this time.

"She might be, but I can't be sure."

"But you think she is, so that's enough." It was Jessica's turn to go quiet for a moment. "There's one way we could find out."

"You mean, by asking her?"

Jessica nodded.

"Are you really sure you wanna do that?" Jared asked.

"Do we have a choice?"

Another thought struck him. "What are you gonna tell your mom when she sees you off college?"

"Guess I'll have to think of something. We gotta ask her, anyway."

"Okay. Will we go there now?"

"Mom's working, but she's free at seven this evening. We'll do

45

it then."

Jared placed a reassuring hand on her right shoulder. "Whatever you decide, I'll be behind you."

"Thanks, Jared." Jessica leaned over and hugged him.

***

Bertha sat in her office, holding a ham-and-tuna sandwich. She had an hour for her lunch break and just loved the quiet time.

She swallowed the last bite, washing the bread down with some coffee. In earlier days, Bertha might have been tempted to follow it with a chocolate bar; but she hadn't felt much of a need for them since she'd gotten on track with a healthier lifestyle.

Bringing the hot mug up to her lips, Bertha was about to drink some more coffee when the phone rang.

Not answering it. I'm on my break.

As she pulled out a magazine from one of the drawers in her desk, the phone trilled again.

Bertha sighed and picked up the receiver. *Just in case it's serious.*

"Hello?"

There was silence on the other end.

"Hello? Anyone there?"

Again, she was met with no answer.

"Look, if this is someone's idea of a prank call—"

The unexpected sound of loud static and crackling noises made her stop. Garbled voices clamored in unison.

"Is someone there?" Bertha asked, raising her voice in annoyance.

"Homi ..." a woman said above the din.

"What's that?" Bertha's patience was quickly waning.

The static cleared, and the caller spoke, their tone chilling and distorted. *"Homicidium!"*

Bertha dropped the receiver and jumped back a little. Her face turned ashen and heart raced. With a trembling hand, she scooped up the phone.

"Wh—Who is this?"

The voices rose again, joining in a chorus of manic laughter that made Bertha bolt outside.

She lit up a cigarette, taking the first drag and blowing out a blue plume of smoke.

What was that call about? she thought as her pulse slowed. *What's "homicidium"?*

For ten minutes, Bertha stood smoking, watching cars go by and women going for a walk with their prams.

She was still a little shaken up, so she decided to wash up in the ladies' bathroom. Sometimes, when she was stressed after her ex-husband, Bill, had left, Bertha loved to splash cold water on her face, imagining that each drop that sluiced off was an ounce of frustration fading away. She stayed bent over the sink for a moment; then, snapping a piece of hand towel from the roll, she dried herself off.

Bertha froze while raising her head. In the mirror to her far right, there was a reflection of a young woman, wearing denim shorts and a blouse and with long black hair falling over her face, staring back at her. The woman's eyes were wide and wild with fury.

Bertha's breath grew shaky as the intruder slowly raised a hand, pointing an accusatory finger at her.

"Homicidium!" the woman cried. She screamed, and the light-bulb above Bertha exploded. It was Bertha's turn to yell in terror, cowering next to the sink in the fetal position and covering her head with both hands as she sobbed away.

When a few minutes had passed, Bertha braved a peek through her fingers. The angry woman was gone. Composing herself, Bertha got to her feet and dashed out of the toilets.

Was I seeing things? Was that really her?

***

Jessica sat in her motel room listening to the radio. For the last half hour, she had been pacing the floor, working up the courage to ring her mom. Since meeting Jared this morning, Bertha had been on her mind. Jessica wondered what this ghost had planned. Was her mom going to be attacked, like Jared and herself had been attacked by Caleb and the demon over a year ago?

Scrolling through her contacts, Jessica tapped her mother's name. She laid the phone down on the bed and put it on loud-speaker.

"Hey there, honey," Bertha greeted, stress evident in her voice. The radio blared—the same station Jessica had just been listening to—but the volume soon dimmed. "How was college today?"

"Not bad. You know, the usual. Are you finished with work? Are you okay?"

"Yup, busy day. Just got home ten minutes ago. Gonna put my feet up now and watch some TV."

"Cool. Um, Mom, there's something I have to tell you."

"It sounds serious. Are you in trouble? Don't tell me you're pregnant!"

"No, God no. It's just—" Jessica was interrupted by a *blip* sound. "Hold on a second, Mom."

A text message from Jared had just come in. Jessica opened it. *Play the news. Now!*

"I'm still here, Mom," she said. "Just a second."

Jessica turned up her radio.

"—details of the victim have been released. This is what Detective Dan Ramirez, heading up the investigation, had to say earlier this morning."

A recording played of the detective reading out a statement.

"Today, we were able to ascertain, through DNA testing, that the body found at the construction site is that of a 24-year-old female. We have identified her as Ms. Tabitha Logan, declared a missing person in 2012 ..."

Jessica stared at the dials, transfixed. The rest of Ramirez's words faded out as she recovered from hearing Tabitha's name. Then she remembered her mother.

"Sorry, Mom," she said. "Are you there?"

Only the sound of the radio playing in Bertha's kitchen.

"Mom?"

"Uh ... um ...sorry, I ... I dropped my phone, there," Bertha replied, sounding rattled.

"Is everything all right? Did something happen?"

"No ... uh ... all good, honey. Sorry, but I gotta go."

Bertha hung up.

"Yeah, we're definitely going to Mom's now," Jessica muttered. She grabbed her keys and phone, turning off the radio and lights.

Gonna call Jared on the way. I need him.

***

Jessica sat in Jared's car, shoulders rigid and sweat running down her forehead. She'd have driven here herself, but wanted a quick talk with her friend before going into the house.

Jared didn't envy what she was about to do. He'd been in a similar position when he had to tell his parents about Caleb and the demon, haunting them.

"How am I gonna do this? I mean, she's gonna kill me," Jessica said, gazing at her hands.

"If you're worried about not being in college ... no offence, Jess, but that's the least of your worries. There's a possibility your mom could be in danger if we don't find out what happened in 2012."

"Yeah, but how am I supposed to bring it up?"

"Well she's gonna want to know why you're here and not on campus. So that'll start the conversation."

"Guess you're right." Jessica sighed, opening the passenger door. "Come on, then. Let's get this over with."

Both of them got out of his car and approached Bertha's front door. Taking a deep breath, Jessica braced herself while ringing the doorbell.

An astonished-looking Bertha stood there, staring at the two teens for a moment.

"Jess, what are you doing here? How come you're not in college?"

"Well, when we were talking on the phone, I thought something was wrong because you sounded scared … so, I came."

Bertha arched an eyebrow in bemusement. "Really? How? By rocket, or did the Enterprise beam you over? Last time I checked, it takes an hour to drive from there to here, and we were only talking twenty minutes ago."

"Fine. I didn't go back. Can we come in? There's something we gotta talk about."

Bertha's expression turned to one of fear, her brows knitting together.

"Okay, sure, come on in." She stood aside.

Jared followed his friend into the kitchen. Part of him wished that he didn't have to be here, but he knew Jessica was in a tough situation. She needed all the support she could get.

"Coffee, anyone?" Bertha asked.

Jessica and Jared shook their heads.

Bertha switched on the kettle to make a cup for herself. "So, what's this about?"

Jessica looked over at Jared and he nodded. Now it was time for the truth.

"The night before I was supposed to go back," Jessica began, "something weird happened. I had a dream that a girl was standing in your room. She was holding a knife. Next thing, she just stabbed you. I woke up and went to the bathroom. When I came back, there was a knife in my pillow, the same kind the girl had in my dream."

"God, Jess! Why am I only hearing about this *now?*"

"Because I thought you'd think I was crazy."

"I'd never think that! What did this girl look like?"

"Um, she had long black hair, and she wore denim shorts and a white blouse …"

Jared noticed the blood draining from Bertha's face, her eyes widening. He guessed Jessica had also seen her mom's reaction when she asked, "Do you know her?"

Bertha sighed and pulled up a chair at the table. She sat, letting out a long exhale, almost as if a huge weight was lifted off her shoulders.

"Since we're being honest—yeah, she does sound familiar, because ... because I've seen her too. Mostly at work."

"Did she say or do anything?" Jared asked.

"Why? What does it matter?" Bertha replied.

"Full disclosure, there's something we gotta talk about, Mom."

For the next ten minutes, Jessica explained about the Caleb Hammerson haunting and Jared's abilities. Bertha, slack-jawed, just nodded, looking at Jared as if he were a complete stranger.

"So you can see the dead?" Bertha asked.

Jared nodded.

"And you saw this girl too?"

He nodded again.

"Did she tell you anything?"

"Did she say anything to you?" Jared deflected, first wanting to find the words to break the news that Tabitha wanted revenge.

"She just said something like ... 'homocidum'? 'Homicidium'?"

"That sounds a lot like homicide." Jessica leaned back in her chair, fixing Bertha with a stern stare. "Is there something you're not telling us?"

"Whoa, Jess," Jared broke in. "Let's take it easy for a moment. I'll Google that. Do you know how to spell it?" he asked Bertha.

"Do I look like a friggin' dictionary?" Bertha joked.

"Okay. Point taken." Jared kept repeating the word, trying to detect what language it was in. "Sounds like Latin or Italian." Jared typed it into his phone, clicking on the alternative spelling Google provided.

He felt a lump in his throat.

"What's wrong?" Jessica asked.

"Um...are you sure she said 'homicidium'?" he said to Bertha.

"Uh-huh. No mistaking that."

"Then ... according to this, she's saying you murdered her."

Jessica lowered her head for a moment, letting out a sigh of exasperation. She reached out a hand for Jared's phone.

"Can I see that?"

Jared handed it to her.

A frown slowly formed on her face. "He's right. That's what it says." Passing it back to him, she continued: "There *is* something you're not telling me and Jared, Mom. Now would be the time to 'fess up."

"Jess's right, Mrs. Barlow. We can't help if you're not honest with us."

Bertha's shoulders slouched and her chin lowered to her chest. She pressed both hands to her cheeks. Tears began to fill her green eyes.

"I suppose I've lived with this secret long enough. I know that girl. Well, me and your dad know her, because ..." Her voice quivered.

Jessica held her mother's hand in encouragement.

"Your dad and I did something terrible back in 2012. It's why we broke up."

Wiping her cheeks, Bertha sat back into the chair. "I was a little tipsy. I'd had a few glasses of wine at your grandma's. Your father was driving us back home that night ..."

***

August 2012

Bill and Bertha were singing along to their 1980s power ballad CD. Van Halen's "Jump" had just finished, and they both started laughing.

"Man, that song never gets old," Bill remarked. "Still as good today as it was in '86!"

"Me and my friends used to jump around my room listening to that when Ma and Pa were out." Bertha gave a nostalgic sigh. "God, I miss those days. Everything was simpler back then."

"Sure was."

"When we used to talk about boys we liked."

"I bet you did."

Bertha glanced over at Bill. He still had his youthful good looks, although a few gray ribs had snuck in at the edges of his side-combed brown hair, and those dreamy amber eyes made her swoon just as much as they had when she'd first met him.

"You look handsome today," Bertha said. "I remember that night in Tulsa. I was the envy of *all* my girlfriends." Bertha raised her head and said in a proud voice, "I got there first. Haven't looked back since."

"That's good to know. How many glasses did you have again?"

"Does it matter?" Bertha stretched out her hand, reaching inside his shirt, letting her fingers rove over the bristles of his hairy chest. "You feelin' frisky?"

"Bertha, cut it out. I'm driving."

"Aw, come on, honey. It's been weeks since we ... you know ..."

"Well, we're not doing anything now."

Bertha withdrew her hand and moved to stroking his cheeks instead. "Mmm ... lookin' good tonight, darlin'."

"Will you stop! I'm—"

The lights of a parked car on a tight bend made Bill swerve to the right. He and Bertha screamed as they hit something. A heavy thud on the windshield, and then the roof, confirmed their worst fears.

Braking hard, Bill brought the vehicle to a halt. They sat in dazed horror, staring out through the cracked windshield, unable to speak. Bertha slowly glanced into the rear-view mirror. A black outline, highlighted by the other car's headlights, caught her attention.

"Oh m—my God, Bill. I—I think w—we hit someone," she stuttered. The surreal moment made all her drunkenness disappear. She was alert, no longer prone to silly talk.

Bill turned off the CD. "Yeah, we did."

"Are you gonna check to see if they're ...?" Bertha couldn't bring herself to say it. Even the thought was too much to bear.

"Um ..." Bill tried to speak, but his voice was shaky and disbelieving. His hands trembled. A few times, he attempted to look into the mirror, but couldn't. "Wai—Wait he—here while I ..."

"Yeah."

Bill opened the door and closed his eyes. Bertha could see, through his clenched fist and quiet mumbling, that he was psyching himself up to go investigate.

Holding on to the roof to steady himself, Bill got out and took a few steps.

"Oh shit!" he blurted.

"What?"

"It's a girl. I think she's ... she's ..."

"Oh, Christ." Bertha's own hands began to tremble.

"Gonna take ... a closer look."

In the rear-view mirror, Bertha saw him walking towards the body, which was lying on its side, facing their car. There was no movement. When he reached the girl, Bill put a hand up to his mouth in shock. He gripped his hair in despair. He rushed to the nearest bush, vomiting into it. Bill stayed bent over, hands on his knees. Eventually, he straightened up, wiped his mouth and slowly walked back to Bertha.

Bill sank into the driver's seat, paler than any white sheet they had at home.

"Is ... she ...?" Bertha asked.

Bill nodded. His eyes bulged in total consternation. "We ... We got to phone ... an ambulance ... police ... somebody ..."

"No, we can't. They'll ... arrest us if we do."

"We can't just leave that girl there! Somebody else is bound to find her, and then what?"

"I ... well ... " Bertha had to think fast. The longer they were there, the bigger the chance someone would come along, put two and two together. "If we phone the cops, they'll arrest us for reckless driving and murder! Who's gonna look after Jess then?"

"But it was an accident."

"They're not gonna care, Bill!"

Bertha stayed silent for a moment, letting that thought sink in.

"What are we gonna do so?" he asked.

"We have to move the body."

"How?"

"Put her in the trunk, backseat, I don't know," she spat back.

"Well, excuse me. I just killed someone! It's not like I do it every God damn day," Bill snapped.

He and Bertha grew quiet again, each gathering themselves and calming down.

"Something has to be done, and fast," Bill reminded her.

"Thanks for pointing out the obvious." Bill threw Bertha a fiery glance. "Sorry," she sighed. "Okay, here's what we're gonna do …"

Present Day

"So we put Tabitha in the trunk and buried her in a field half a mile away. Nobody ever used it ... until they started building there recently. Your father went back and picked up her car. By that time, I'd sobered up, and I took our car to Branson Lake, where he dumped Tabitha's vehicle." Bertha took a mouthful of coffee and wiped away some tears streaking her cheeks. "I couldn't sleep for weeks. A month later, your father started sleeping in the spare room. We prayed nobody would find her. Guess that was too much to hope for, huh?"

A stupefied Jared and Jessica just stared wide-eyed at Bertha.

"Now everything makes sense—all those arguments you guys had, why Dad spent less time here. All along, I thought it was something I did," Jessica said.

Bertha moved her chair next to Jessica's. She put an arm around her.

"Oh, honey, I'm so sorry you thought that. I never wanted that to happen. There were many times I wanted to tell you the truth; but if I did, it would've meant trouble for all of us."

"Why didn't Daddy ever reach out to me, then?"

"Maybe he felt he couldn't. I don't know."

Lights flickered before a churning feeling rumbled in Jared's stomach. This meant only one thing.

"Uh, guys, I think we got company," he announced.

"Do you mean she's here?" Jessica asked.

Jared tried with all his might to not jump out of his chair when Tabitha emerged from the wall behind where Bertha and Jessica sat. She had a baleful expression, and her eyes, filled with hatred, fixed on one person.

"She is now," he replied.

Both women jumped, glancing around in horror.

"Where?" Jessica asked.

Tabitha, balling her fists, stood beside Bertha. The dead woman's face was contorted in anger.

"I ... don't think you wanna know," Jared replied. He focused his attention on Tabitha. "Don't hurt anyone here, all right?"

"Since you're the messenger, pass this along," she said, each word said through gritted teeth. "Tell her she has forty-eight hours to turn herself in."

Jared repeated to Bertha what the ghost told him.

"What happens if I don't?" Bertha asked.

"Your daughter will be without a mother like mine was ... *is*," Tabitha warned.

"She said ..." Jared was hesitant, but there was no other way to phrase it. "If you don't, Jessica won't have a mom."

"If I turn myself in she won't have one, either! Look, I'm so sorry about what happened to you. We never meant for you to get hurt. It was an accident."

"An *accident?*" Tabitha exclaimed.

All eyes shifted to the table as Bertha's mug, which had a little coffee still left in it, wobbled and spun around. Bertha, Jessica, and Jared backed away before it exploded, the hot black liquid spraying everywhere. They screamed and ducked.

Tabitha remained standing. Fury lurked in her pupils, which were now trained on Bertha. "You left me to die and then buried me like I was a pile of garbage! So I will have justice, one way or another."

Jared repeated the warning.

Tabitha looked at Jessica for a few seconds before reverting her attention to Bertha. "Make sure you tell her this. If she doesn't do what I say"—Tabitha stayed focused on Jessica—"she's gonna lose something precious too."

"Wait? Is that a threat?" Jared said.

Tabitha disappeared.

Bertha stepped forward, having read the concern on his face. "What did she say?"

"We gotta figure something out, and fast," Jared said, trying to avoid the question. A million thoughts ran through his head.

"Jared, what did she say?" Bertha demanded.

"If you don't do what she says, Jessica is going to get hurt."

"So is she coming after me or Jessica?"

Jared was too busy thinking to answer.

A deafening silence fell on them as they all sat down, the gravity of this situation hitting everyone.

"Don't worry, Jessica honey. We'll think of something," Bertha said.

I hope so, Jared thought. "It might be safer if you guys stay somewhere else for a few nights."

"Like where, a motel?" Jessica said.

"Yeah. Anywhere but here. It will make you harder to find and might buy us some time."

"Jared's right." Bertha grabbed Jessica's hand. "Come on. Help me pack. We'll get enough clothes for a few days."

From his experience, Jared knew that Tabitha wasn't joking. A vengeful spirit was the worst kind to take on. Sooner or later, if something wasn't done, somebody was going to suffer—or worse, die.

***

Jared helped Jessica and Bertha bring their suitcases into the motel room, which was painted a light pink and had two single beds. A picture of a dilapidated shotgun shack hung on the near wall. Jessica had checked herself out of the other motel earlier before join-ing Bertha in this one.

"Is that all?" Jared asked while putting down a case and mas-saging his wrists.

Bertha scanned the bags. "Yeah, I think that's everything. Thanks."

"No problem. I have to get something from the car. Be back in a sec."

Jessica waited until her friend left the room before asking, "Do you think we'll be here for long?"

"I hope not. Don't get me wrong, I regret every day how that poor girl died—but part of me hopes Jared can get rid of her. Help her cross over, or something."

"You gotta see it from her side too, Mom. She was *killed*. Tabi-tha's family will never see her again. Of course she's going to want payback!"

"If it were as simple as me turning myself in, I'd do it, but I can't. You'll need me. You're still a young girl."

Jared returned with a can of pure salt. He stuck one of his car keys under the lid and popped it open.

"Okay, pay attention, because this will keep out any spirits." He took a pinch of salt out of the can, scattering in front of the door. "Do the same on the window sills and all four corners of this room. Do it in the morning, and before you go to sleep." He reached into his back jeans pocket and took out a crumpled-up piece of paper. "Say this protection prayer before you leave here—and at night, too."

"How do you know the salt and prayer will work?" Bertha asked.

"Trust me, they do," Jessica reassured her.

"I'm going to phone my Aunt Belle," Jared said. "She taught me everything. I'll ask if there's a way we can trap Tabitha. Keep your phones on. I'll be in touch tomorrow morning again. Night."

"Night, Jared," both women said as he walked out the door, closing it behind him.

"So, while he's figuring out what he's gonna do, we have to talk about our next move," Jessica said.

"I don't know, Jess. I mean, what can we do? I'm not turning myself in. That's off the table."

"If you don't, or dad doesn't, then someone is going to die. Why can't you see that?"

"Maybe Jared will figure something out. There mightn't be any need for anyone to go to the cops."

"If Jared can't come up with something, what then? We need to have a backup plan—and in case you've forgotten, we've only got forty-eight hours," Jessica pointed out.

"I know, I know. Let me think it over tonight, and then we'll decide in the morning. Okay?"

Jessica sighed and nodded.

"Great. Thanks. Now, let's just unpack and get some sleep."

As Jessica took out some clothes and decided what to wear tomorrow, that butterfly fluttering feeling in her stomach returned. She knew Jared had come through in the past; but right now, there didn't appear to be any way to get out of this unscathed. *Somebody* was going to have to pay. Two terrifying questions remained in her mind: who would be the victim, and what price would they ultimately have to pay?

***

Bertha hummed a song she had heard earlier as she made her way to the car. Her shift was finally over, and she was relieved to be returning to the motel.

Bertha shut the door and rolled down her window. There was time for one more cigarette.

Never had she smoked as much as in the last week. The haunting was hitting Bertha's nerves hard, and smoking was the only thing that made her feel at ease. Drinking wasn't an option for her any longer.

Bertha took a drag of her cigarette before turning on the radio. A jubilant female reporter read out the headlines. Bertha didn't pay much attention until a story about Tabitha began to play. She turned up the volume.

"Today, we spoke to Mrs. Imelda Logan about her daughter's case being re-opened. This is what she had to say." There was a slight pause before the grief-stricken mother spoke.

"I'm so grateful to Detective Ramirez and the Hopps Town PD for all they're doing. The last eight years have been ..." Her voice wavered and she caught a breath. "... have been tough on our family. Every day I have to look at my grand-daughter and face the reality that she'll never see her mom again. No child ..." Imelda began to sob.

Bertha's heart sank, and she found her own eyes welling up.

Mrs. Logan continued. "Sorry. No child should have to be without a mom. I hope Detective Ramirez finally catches whoever did this," Imelda paused again, trying to compose herself. "Bring this family the closure we deserve—and that Tabitha, my little baby, can rest in peace."

"Is there anything you want to say to those responsible for Tabitha's death?" the interviewer asked.

Imelda cleared her throat, speaking with a firm tone. "Do the right thing and turn yourself in. End this, for all of us."

Bertha turned the radio off, hearing enough. Her vision blurred. For so long, she'd wanted to do something, but she was afraid. Not just because it would have meant Jessica being put into the foster system—she was afraid of going to prison, too. In this state, they didn't have the death penalty for murderers. Still, Bertha knew there was a high probability that she'd be in there for the rest of her days, missing out on Jessica's special moments, like getting married and having kids of her own.

Images of Tabitha being a passive observer to her own daughter's triumphs, never being able to be involved in them, came like punches to Bertha's gut.

Bertha threw out the cigarette, leaning forward on the steering wheel. Her whole body shook as she cried.

"I'm so sorry, Tabitha," she spluttered out, now reduced to a blubbering mess. "I don't know how to make this right."

For another five minutes, Bertha continued to sob heavily. Her eyes roved over the parking lot to check if anyone was staring or could see her in this state. No-one was around, and she sighed in relief.

***

The warm tea worked its way down Bertha's throat as she drank the last of what was in her favorite cup.

Got to get another in a minute, she thought. Bertha had just pressed send on an email when a knock came to her office door.

"Who is it?" she asked.

"We got a problem outside," Norman replied.

"What kind of problem?" Norman didn't answer. "Norm, you there?"

Again, silence. Cursing him under her breath, Bertha got up to investigate.

The store was unusually quiet for this time of day. All the aisles were empty. There weren't any half-stocked shopping carts parked precariously or customers standing around chatting to one another.

"Norm, where are you?" Bertha called out. *Might have gone out for a smoke,* she told herself.

A tapping sound made her turn around. The juice inside the pickle jars behind her bubbled up like boiling water, and the pickles transformed into blinking eyeballs, tracing Bertha's every movement. She started retreating as the liquid became blood-red.

In a flash, jars launched off the shelf, flying over her head and zipping past her. She screamed and ran to the office as more crashed off the wall or on the ground inches behind her.

Slamming the office door, Bertha pressed her back to it to keep it firmly shut. She closed her eyes and rattled off a prayer, begging for this madness to stop.

An odor of rotten eggs invaded the room. Bertha's nose crinkled in disgust. She covered it with a tissue that was in her pocket.

"That's gross," she mumbled. Bertha opened the window wide and ran back to the door.

Without warning, a hand shot through it, covering her mouth. Bertha's screams were muffled as an all-too-familiar, sinister voice spoke.

"Want this to stop? You know what to do," Tabitha snarled.

Bertha gasped as she sat up. She had fallen asleep on her desk, but the dream was too real to be dismissed.

There was only one person who might be able to get them out of this but Bertha wondered if he would even respond. She hoped that he would when all their lives hung in the balance.

***

Jared stood in the long line of people waiting to be served at Maisy's Bagels. Hers were the best in Hopps Town, especially the bacon and melted cheese sandwiched in a warm, crispy bun. That, along with a chai latte, always set him up for the day.

There were three rows of tables, and pictures of famous writers, alongside lifelike portraits of complete strangers, hung on both sides of Maisy's store. Jared never really understood her decor style, but the food more than made up for it.

As he got closer to the counter, Jared glanced around. A man with neatly combed ginger hair and wearing a pin-striped suit, who was sat drinking herbal tea, caught his attention. He reminded Jared of an extra-suave Bond villain.

The man noticed him staring and gave a friendly smile. There was something about him that the boy didn't like, and the hairs on Jared's arms stood up. He looked elsewhere, but he could still feel the man studying him.

As Jared was leaving, the suave stranger nodded to him in greeting. Jared walked faster.

What's up with that guy? he thought.

The smell of bacon wafted its way up from the plastic bag, making Jared's stomach rumble with hunger. He set it down to take out his car key. Some change spilled out of his pocket, and he bent down to pick it up. When he straightened, Jared jumped back.

The man in the suit was standing just a few feet from him.

"Hello," the stranger said.

"Uh ... hi," Jared replied, quickly pressing the button to unlock his car door.

"Tabitha. She's ours, you know."

Jared stared at him, perplexed. "Wha—What do you mean, sir?"

"Oh, I think you know what I mean." The man's eyes glowed a menacing red.

Jared almost recoiled again. The stranger was gone. Jared knew he was a demon.

Hot damn, not another one. It's like Caleb Hammerson all over again!

After wiping his hands and retrieving his bagel, he got into the car.

"I'm gonna need advice for this."

He called his aunt; and, after three rings, a bubbly, bordering-on-giddy Maybelle answered. "Hey, Sam, how ya doin'?

"'Sam'? Aunt Belle, it's me, Jared."

"I know that. I meant like the Winchester brothers. *Supernatural*? Last time we met, I called dibs on Dean, remember?"

"Oh, that, yeah. Except *I'm* Dean."

"Since I'm your aunt and older, I get to be him."

"Sure, whatever. For a lady who broke her ankle, you sound really chirpy."

"Must be the morphine kicking in. So, what can I do for ya?"

Jared took a bite of the bacon-and-cheese goodness. "We've a problem here. Can't say too much over the phone, but it's a double whammy again—demon and ghost working together."

"Oh, crap. Do you know why this person's being haunted by both?"

Jared gave a very brief overview of the current scenario, without mentioning names. Maybelle fell silent for a moment. He knew she was choosing her words carefully, so as not to scare him.

"This is a tricky one, J—much trickier than the Hammerson case. That ghost has a good reason to be pissed off. It's possible that her spirit was disturbed by the construction. If she's out for re-venge and has a demon's help, anything can happen at any time. Be aware of that, all right?"

"Uh-huh. Could really use you here, Belle. Feels like too much to handle. It's not a simple crossing-over."

"Told you before, J: these kind of cases are gonna come your way all throughout your life."

"What should I do?"

"Have you tried reasoning with this spirit?"

"I think she's beyond that." He took another bite.

"I thought that. All right. You gotta do what we did last year, get them to one place and banish 'em."

"Sounds easy, but it ain't."

"You got this. I believe in you." There was a slight pause be-fore she spoke again, more hurriedly. "Looks like the nice nurse is coming to give some more painkillers. Yeah, I just love me some morphine. Woohoo!"

A broad smile crept across his face, imagining Maybelle doing a little dance in her hospital bed. "Sounds like you have a fun evening ahead."

"Oh, sure! My leg's in a sling and I'm in a ward on my own. What more can a girl want? I gotta go. Nurse Betty here's giving me funny looks. Talk later, and don't worry—"

"I know, I got this. Take care, Belle. Love ya."

"Back at ya, nephew."

Jared hung up and locked his phone. In his mind, there were only two ways to end this: risk Bertha being packed off to jail, or do what Maybelle suggested. He hoped both Jessica and Bertha would be open to it.

**

Jessica, with pen in hand and a notepad in front of her, took notes as she watched a YouTube video one of her college professors had recommended. Her phone pinged with a text from Jared.

Are you at the motel?

Jessica replied that she was.

Three knocks on the door made her jump. Peeping out the window, she sighed in relief when she saw that it was Jared.

She opened the door to let him in, and her eyebrows drew together when she saw the look on Jared's face. "What's wrong?"

"We gotta talk. Something weird just happened." Pointing to the sandwich he said, "Do you mind if I eat this here?"

"No, go ahead."

Jared sat on Bertha's bed.

"So what happened?" Jessica asked. "You look pretty shook up."

Jared chewed some of the bagel. "Dang, this is good." Swallowing, he continued. "I went to Maisy's. There was a weird dude there—something about him was off. I got back to my car and dropped some quarters, and then he appears out of nowhere while I'm picking them up. The guy's eyes went red, like, cherry-red."

"Wait, are you saying he was a ...?"

"Demon? Yup. Sure was." He took another bite of his sandwich.

"Did he say anything?"

Jared knew she'd ask this question and had an answer prepared. "Yeah. Somebody's gonna get hurt, and soon. Maybelle says we need to do one of two things: either get rid of them like we did last year, or your mom has to turn herself in."

"You know she's not going to do that. Part of me doesn't want her to either. I don't know what to do."

"Well, there's only a little over twenty-four hours left. I could try banishing them like we did at the well, but something tells me your mom won't like that."

"Not a chance. She won't even watch horror movies. Do you think we should phone Mom and get her to come home?"

"Tell you what. Let me finish this and we'll go to her."

"All right."

***

65

Bertha kept herself busy all day at work, trying to put the dire warning out of her mind. Stocking shelves, sweeping the floor, re-filing old receipts in chronological order, deleting out-of-date files on the computer and replying to emails didn't take her mind off of it. Since Tabitha's ultimatum, she had messaged Bill, but had yet to get a response.

There's gotta be another way. But no matter how much she tried to think of something else, no other solution presented itself.

At 1 p.m., Bertha took a lunch break. She sat eating an order of taco fries in her office—times like this made her lapse back into old habits.

With every bite she took, Bill was constantly on her mind. Her parents were never religious or really believed in God, and neither did she. Jessica had asked a while back to go to church, but Bertha had refused. Now she wondered if some deity or celestial being was giving her a hint.

Bertha's eyes kept being drawn to her small, pink cell phone. It may as well have been in a cheerleading outfit and waving pom-poms.

Aw, dammit!

Bertha picked it up. Logging into her Facebook account, she typed in Bill's name. His profile came up underneath five others. After clicking on his picture, her finger hovered for a few minutes over the Message button. Some of those old feelings came rushing back after seeing him again.

Sure still looks handsome, she thought. *Why did it have to be us that night that hit Tabitha? We were so happy.*

With a mournful sigh, Bertha hit the button, typing another message: *Hi Bill. I really need u to txt me back. We need ur help.*

Just hope he answers, she thought.

The afternoon sunshine lifted Bertha's mood a little. Thoughts of Tabitha being around every corner, ready to pounce on her, had been keeping her awake at night; so, she put two dollar coins into the vending machine and a can of soda slid down.

One of the store's doors whined as it opened. Bertha didn't turn around, letting Norman deal with the customer instead.

A man spoke. "Hi. Detective Ramirez, Hopps Town PD. Is Bertha Barlow here?"

Bertha froze, not knowing whether to walk into her office or stay on the store floor.

"She's over there," Norman replied.

Shoot, too late. Smile and act calm. Bertha pulled back the ring on the can.

"Excuse me. Mrs. Barlow?" the detective said.

Bertha offered Ramirez her best friendly, customer-service smile. The man was tall with perfect olive skin and sported a tight crew-cut hairstyle.

"Yes. What can I do for you?" she said.

Ramirez flashed his badge as he replied, "Detective Dan Ramirez, HT PD. I'm just following up on a few leads on the Tabitha Logan case. Do you mind if I ask a few questions?"

"Sure." She held her soda tightly to stop her hand from shaking and took a deep breath to remain calm.

The detective took out a notepad, flipping through some pages before stopping at one. "Can you tell me your whereabouts on August 12th, 2012?"

"Um ... gosh, that's like eight years ago. Hard to remember."

"Please try, ma'am."

"I really don't remember. It was a long time."

"Just try and think back."

Bertha feigned deep thinking, her head low in fake contemplation. "Sorry ... I got nothing. Why do you want to know about that date?"

"I presume you've heard about the Tabitha Logan case?"

"Yeah ... that's the girl whose body was found at the construction site?"

Ramirez nodded.

"Heard it mentioned on the radio," Bertha said. "What about her?"

"She went missing after that night and was never seen again, until her body was discovered recently."

"Okay, but what's all this got to do with me?"

"Did you own a silver 2005 sedan eight years ago?"

"Sounds about right. What of it?"

The detective folded up the notepad and stared at her intently. "We asked all the auto repair shops if any cars came in damaged after August 12th, 2012. Most don't keep records that far back; but lucky for us, one did. Cadwell's Auto Repair said that a car matching the description was brought in with a cracked windshield and a dent to the front. That ring any bells now?"

Bertha had thought about being defensive but decided against it. That might make her look even guiltier. Instead, she said, "Oh, now I remember. I was driving back from my mother's house when a deer ran across the road and I hit it. The poor thing was bleeding pretty bad, but it walked away. Don't ask me how."

"A deer? That's what you're saying you hit?" Ramirez asked with incredulity in his voice.

"Yes, a deer." *No more missus nice girl.* "No offence, Detective, but are you going somewhere with this? Are you trying to accuse me of something?"

"No, just following up on some leads. Did you know Tabitha Logan personally?"

"No, I didn't."

"So you're saying you never met her?"

Bertha shook her head.

"All right. And your husband can corroborate this story?" the detective asked.

"Sure, if you can find him."

"What do you mean?"

"We split up a few months after that accident. Before you ask, no, I don't know where he is now. We don't keep in touch."

"I see." He reached into his dark gray suit jacket and took out a business card, giving it to her. "This is my number. If you remember anything else, give me a call; and if your husband comes back, tell him to get in touch with me." The detective was about to turn away when he paused. "Oh, and one last thing. Don't leave town anytime soon."

"Why, am I a person of interest?"

"Just don't leave town," he replied in a sharp tone.

Bertha hated lying to the police, but she couldn't use Bill as the fall guy, even though it would have been much harder for Ramirez to prove. She reasoned that, at least, if anything happened her, Bill would be around to step in for Jessica. Bertha felt horrible inside for cutting him out of his daughter's life.

That was close. It's bad enough we have a ghost and a demon tormenting us, now we have the cops giving us a hard time, too. We definitely gotta end this, and fast, Bertha thought.

***

Walking into St. Peter's Church made Jessica feel like an imposter. The statues of Jesus, the Virgin Mary, and other saints creeped her out with the way their eyes always seemed to follow your every movement. She lowered her head, avoiding their gazes while walking past them, heading straight for the holy water font. They'd run out of the small amount Jared had given them to sprinkle on the walls and doors, so she scooped up some with an empty plastic milk jug.

As she was about to leave, Jessica stopped, deciding to say a quick prayer. She knelt down at the bottom pew.

"I don't know if anyone is listening," she began. "I kind of feel like a hypocrite doing this, since we never come here. Truth is, we need you: God, Jesus or whoever up there. My mom and dad did a bad thing eight years ago. There's no getting away from that, and we're sorry Tabitha died. Please show us a way out of this without someone getting hurt."

Glancing around, and with her cheeks scarlet from the embarrassment of feeling like she was talking to herself, Jessica quickly got up and walked out.

In her car, Jessica rummaged through the glove compartment for her favorite driving CD.

"Gotcha," Jessica said, putting it into the player. Techno beats pulsed through the speakers as she pulled out onto the road.

She groaned as the traffic lights changed to red, tapping her fingers on the wheel as she waited.

A new tune started playing. Midway through, the singer's voice became distorted.

"Please don't be broken." That would mean another half hour of trying to find this music on the internet, seeing as Jessica forgot to add the tracks to her playlist last time.

Stylish guitar playing was replaced with low growls that reverberated around the car, and she knew it wasn't coming from a scratched CD.

"Oh, hell no," Jessica mumbled, sweat beginning to break out on her back.

Come on, change to green, dammit!

A soft breeze blew across her neck before something yanked her ponytail, hard. Jessica screamed. One quick glance into the rear-view mirror revealed that she was being pulled by an invisible hand.

Its grip tighter grew, forcing Jessica to lie further back in her seat. Tears clouded her vision. Any minute now, she expected her hair to be ripped out of her head. Kicking the dashboard, Jessica screamed once more, writhing and wriggling to break free.

Ice-cold fingers caressing her shoulders and slid all the way to Jessica's mouth, silencing her yelling. A hot breath whispered into her left ear, a slimy tongue slithering across the earlobe.

"Next time, there'll be no mercy. Tick ... tock ... tick ... tock."

Her attacker let go of her.

A long line had formed behind the car. Irate drivers honked their horns, trying to get Jessica to move, while others overtook her. Some stuck their heads out of their windows, shouting obscenities.

With trembling hands and a thumping heart, Jessica pressed the accelerator and pulled over near the sidewalk to compose herself.

I can't go through this again. Not after last year!

Opening the glove compartment, she took out a tissue and

dabbed her eyes.

Come on, get a grip. Don't let them win.

Taking a deep breath, Jessica moved out into the line of traffic, heading back to the motel.

***

Jessica half-stumbled into the room. Nausea almost overcame her, everything spinning around again. She staggered over to a chair and fell into it.

Bertha came out of the bathroom, her face blanched. "Honey, what's wrong?"

"I ... I don't wanna talk about it."

Bertha crouched, catching Jessica's hand. "Something happened. Don't shut me out like this. Talk to me, baby."

On the way back, Jessica had managed to compose herself; but as soon as she had pulled into the parking lot, it hit her like a wrecking ball. Traces of moisture from that slimy tongue, along with the spine-shivering feeling from those frozen fingers, remained. Pain still lingered around the base of her ponytail.

"On my way here, I was ... attacked."

"Do you mean somebody tried to break into your car?"

"No, no. Something pulled my hair, really hard."

"You mean like a ... a ghost?"

"Yeah, but it didn't feel like Tabitha. It's something worse."

"Oh my God. That's *it*. We need to do something, now!" Bertha stood up and grabbed her phone.

"Who're you calling?"

"I'm texting Jared. We need to meet up at Jackie's. This is gonna stop, and I think I know how." She sent the message. "Can I get you anything to calm your nerves? How about a cup of cocoa? That used to help when you were younger."

"That was when I couldn't sleep," Jessica said. "I'm gonna need a drink stronger than that."

Bertha opened up her handbag and took out a herbal remedy. "This should do the trick." She squeezed two drops into a glass of water and gave it to Jessica. "Drink. It will take about ten minutes to kick in."

Jessica regarded it with a skeptical look. "What's in that?"

"Something that will take the edge off. Go on." Bertha gestured with her head. "Don't worry, it ain't gonna bite."

Reluctantly, Jessica drank the water, wincing and grimacing when the sour taste hit. "Thanks ... I think."

Bertha's phone vibrated on the bed. She looked at the screen, which illuminated her face a neon blue, then grabbed her makeup bag.

"Jared said he'd meet us in thirty minutes. Get ready."

All Jessica's worries and uneasiness were being chipped away like a wave working its way up the shore. Bertha insisted Jessica come in her car instead of driving them; and, by the time they drove out of the motel's parking lot, Jessica was relaxed, devoid of any fears.

Wish I could feel like this all the time, she thought.

***

Thoughts of Anna always crossed Tabitha's mind. *What is she doing now? Does she have many friends, maybe even a crush? How's she doing in school? Are her grades good?*

One of Malik's rules was that Tabitha could not interfere with her mother's home, or in her and Anna's lives, in any way. If Tabitha broke that stipulation, he often reminded her, she'd be getting revenge alone. Up until now, Tabitha had honored their agreement; but curiosity got the better of her.

Merely thinking of Imelda's house brought her there. Porcelain gnome statues with toothy grins under bushy white beards stood guard by the door.

"Coming, Grandma!" Tabitha heard Anna shout. Slowly, Tabitha approached the front door, hesitating to enter. Malik's warning played in her mind, almost as if he sensed her intentions.

Dammit, I'm just gonna do it this one time, she thought, taking that tentative first step into the hallway.

Everything was where it used to be. Maybe it was Imelda's way of remembering her, Tabitha reasoned.

Anna—taller, now, with black hair falling halfway down her back, and brown eyes and rosy cheeks like her father—ran down the stairs.

"No running! I don't want you falling and breaking a leg or an arm," Imelda yelled.

"Sorry, Grandma." Anna was the same height Tabitha was at her age. She was blossoming into a beautiful young woman.

You'll be a heartbreaker, Tabitha thought, *and I won't even get to meet your first partner.*

All the other important events that she'd miss out on flashed through her mind. "I'll never get to be there for your prom, or your wedding day." Tabitha clenched her fists. "Never get to see my grandchildren." If she were alive, her palms would be bleeding from her nails digging into them. Tabitha continued through gritted teeth, "All ... because ... of them."

Lights flickered overhead. A mirror close to Tabitha fogged up.

Uh-oh, gotta rein it in. Through teary eyes, she blew Imelda and Anna a kiss.

"Miss you both," she said.

"Peaches, you need to get back here, now!" Malik commanded telepathically.

"Oh, damn."

With only a thought of the black abyss, the ghost was back there within an instant.

Malik sat on a cozy orange sofa in front of a blazing, open-hearth fire. He held a martini in his right hand.

"I thought we had a deal? You wouldn't go back there if I agreed to help you."

"I just had to see them one last time," Tabitha pleaded. "It's hard not being in my daughter's life."

Malik tutted. "Such silly emotions will only get in the way of your revenge. Don't think about Anna or your dear old mom any more. They're the past."

"I know, but—"

73

"No buts." Malik cut her off sharply, knocking back the rest of the drink before throwing the glass into the fire. As he stood up, the fury in his eyes matched the flames' intensity. "If you can't honor our deal, tell me now so no more of my time is wasted. Well?"

Browbeaten, Tabitha was unable to meet his gaze.

"Well?" Malik roared.

"Fine, I won't see them again! Okay?"

He walked calmly to her with both hands clasped behind his back. "If we're to be successful in making those people pay, I have to know you're focused. This won't work otherwise. From now on, do I have your one-hundred-percent commitment?"

"Yeah, of course."

"Good." A fatherly smile erased the anger from Malik's face. "It looks like they haven't turned themselves in."

"What now?"

"We'll give them another forty eight hours to comply."

"And if they don't?"

Malik put an arm around her shoulders. Malevolent joy dripped from every word he spoke. "Then, my dear, we shall have some fun ... and some people are going to get *very* hurt."

***

The waitress brought Jessica her order of nachos and a soda. Jared settled for a milkshake, while Bertha just wanted a double espresso.

"So what's wrong?" Jared asked when Bertha had left to use the restroom. "Your mom sounded serious in her text. Did something happen?"

"Yeah, I was attacked by a ghost in the car," Jessica said.

Jared started coughing and almost choked on his drink.

"Are you okay?" she asked when he stopped.

"Yup. Fine. But are you all right? I mean, obviously you're not hurt but ... you know ..."

"Yeah, I do; and I'm okay. Pretty shaken up, but I'll live."

"So, how exactly did they attack you?" Jared asked.

Jessica explained how she was assaulted earlier.

"Whoa, that's some nasty stuff. Kinda reminds me of when Caleb tried to choke me last year. But that sounds like a demon instead of a ghost. Ghosts don't usually … lick people's ears. You did sprinkle holy water in the car, right?"

"Well ..." Jessica's gaze fell to the table. "No, I didn't. I was on my way to the motel, but I forgot to do that."

"That's why you need to do it, Jess. Always be careful, especially since we got a ghost who wants revenge and has a demon helping her."

Bertha emerged from the toilet and sat down, making a welcome observation. "Oh, they gave me a free cookie this time. Yay!" She took a bite out of it and drank some of her coffee. "So, has Jess brought you up to speed?"

"Uh-huh. I know we gotta do something—but the easier option, and don't shoot the messenger here, would be for somebody to turn themselves in."

"Jared." Bertha let out a sigh of frustration. "We've been over this. I feel bad every day about what went down back then. Every. Single. Day. But I'm not about to abandon my baby girl."

"Mom!" Jessica protested, both annoyed and embarrassed at being made feel like a child.

"Well it's true. You'll always be my baby. There has to be another way."

It was Jared's turn to exhale, releasing some of his own annoyance. "There is, but it's not gonna be easy. Truth be told, Mrs. B, it's gonna scare the crap outta you."

"Why?" Bertha asked.

"Remember what we told you about the exorcism we did at the well?" he asked.

It took a few seconds for Bertha to realize that this was option B. "Oh, God. That's the only other idea you can come up with?"

"'Fraid so," Jared replied.

A bell rang as another customer came in. Bertha's eyes lit up and a hopeful smile smoothed the creases on her forehead that were there a few seconds ago.

Jessica noticed this and turned around. The girl went rigid, a look of puzzlement on her freckled face.

Sliding out of her seat, Jessica stood up. Her expression of confusion was now replaced with disbelief as she took a few steps toward the man.

"D—Dad?"

PART FOUR: BIG TROUBLE IN HOPPS TOWN

Jessica didn't know whether to laugh or cry. Shock numbed her.

"Dad? Is that really you?"

"It is." Bill was exactly as she remembered him, save for a little more gray hair at the sides of his head. His eyes still twinkled. She could see from his awkward stance that he, too, didn't know what to do.

"Why ... why come back now? After all this time?" Jessica asked.

"Your mom reached out and said you needed me."

"I've *needed* you for the last eight years. We both did!"

"Cupcake, listen—"

That was a nickname she missed hearing; but now, it only stirred up more feelings of hatred. "No. You don't get to call me that anymore."

"Jess, things happened ... I'm sure Mom told you."

"Yeah, but she also told me that you had an affair with a wait-ress! How could you?"

Shame caused Bill to look away for a long moment. "I did, and that's something I regret every day. Can we talk outside?"

With folded arms, Jessica threw him an icy stare.

"Please?" Bill pleaded, with those eyes that would melt a heart made of stone.

"Fine. Two minutes," she said.

Bill opened the door, letting her out first. They went and stood next to Bertha's car.

"So how come it took a crisis to hear from you?" Jessica said.

"Things were complicated. I'm guessing by now you know about the accident?"

"Oh, in more ways than one."

"Your mom's text said it was urgent. Are you guys in trouble?"

"Yeah, sort of. But I wanna know why didn't you write or send any cards. Are you ... ashamed of me?"

"Is that what you thought?" Bill let out a curse. "Unbelievable. I'm shocked."

"What? Am I not supposed to be angry?"

"That's not what I mean." He placed a hand on Jessica's shoulder. "I've been sending Christmas and birthday cards every year. Your mother obviously hid them."

"Don't pin this on Mom! She took care of me while you were off doing ... whatever."

"After the accident, things went downhill fast. I left because *she* wanted me to."

Jessica averted her gaze, with a slow, disbelieving headshake and trembling chin. "So she hid those, all this time?"

Bill nodded. "Looks like it."

"Damn her! She had no right." She walked a short distance away with hands on both hips, her back facing Bill. Jessica took a slow, deep breath. "What did she say to get you here?"

"Your mom contacted me on Facebook. Said you guys were in trouble and could I come immediately."

"She wasn't lying about the trouble part."

"Now that I'm here, can you please tell me just what the heck's going on?" Bill asked.

"Sure, but I think you better come inside. Everything will be explained."

Jessica walked in a semi-frustrated stride, swinging back the door. Bill followed her in. She sat in the booth, moving over to make room for her father.

"Everything all right?" Bertha asked.

"Me and you are gonna talk later," Jessica warned her mother. "But right now, Dad needs to know everything."

"Thanks for coming, Bill," Bertha said with a weak, appreciative smile.

"Anything for my little girl," he replied.

Jessica went scarlet, rolling her eyes. "Not that small anymore."

"It's been a while. You look good," Bertha complimented him.

"Thanks. You don't look too shabby, either."

"Okay, guys, I hate to break up this moment," Jared said, "but we need to talk about ... the problem." He paused, surveying nearby tables to make sure nobody would eavesdrop. In a low voice, he told Bill about his gift and all that had occurred.

Bill just sat there, his eyes blinking dumbly and sporting a blank expression. His face paled a little. "Is this some kind of sick joke?" he asked Jared before directing his next question at Bertha. "And you're buying all this?"

"It's real, Bill. Believe me," she snapped back.

"Guys, come on. You really believe in all that spooky supernatural crap?" he said to the group.

"I know how it sounds, but it's true," Jared answered.

"Seriously. You expect me to believe that all this happened?" Bill said again with more incredulity.

Jessica nodded.

Bill looked at everyone before getting up. "I gotta get some air."

Jared was about to follow him when Jessica put up a hand. "No, let me."

She walked out, finding Bill standing beside his blue Buick.

"You okay, Dad?"

"I don't know if this is some joke or—"

"Hold on a minute. Do you actually believe we'd pull something like this just to bring you back here?"

"Come on, Jess, really? This stuff is actually happening?"

Jessica nodded, a look of sadness creeping into her features. She saw Bill's expression change immediately.

"My God, you really *are* telling the truth." Bill's face was now filled with shame. "Geez. Sorry, Jess. I ... I don't know what to say." He hugged his daughter, kissing her head. "I'm sorry you guys are going through this."

Jessica smiled, enjoying his embrace, basking in the moment. This was something she'd wanted for nearly a decade.

"Can we go inside now and finish the conversation?" Jessica asked.

"Sure. Come on."

They sat down again with the others.

"Are we good?" Jared asked.

"Yeah … sorry I didn't believe you," Bill said.

"It's a lot to take in, I know," Bertha said.

Two other customers came in and sat in the booth just below theirs.

"I think we better head back to the motel to talk more about this," Bertha suggested, eyeing the couple that had just come in.

Jessica looked over her shoulder and then back at her mom. "Yeah, good idea."

They gave Bill the address and room number, and he followed them there.

Jared wondered what was said between Jessica and her father. Ever since she came back from talking to him, the tension between the three Barlows was palpable. He knew that seeing Bill for the first time in eight years was an overwhelming shock for her—if he hadn't seen his dad, Oscar, for that time, Jared would want some answers, too. But this was different.

Now, he was sitting in the middle of Jessica and Bertha's motel room, partly wishing he could be somewhere else. Every now and again, Jessica would present Bertha with a frosty glance while she made coffee or tea for everyone.

"Okay, now that we're away from the diner, I think we should explain to Mr. Barlow what needs to be done." Jared took a glass of soda from Jessica and thanked her. "Does anyone want to go over option A?"

"What's that?" Bill asked.

Jared quickly explained that someone turning themselves in might appease the spirit.

"Look, I feel as bad as anyone here about Tabitha's death, but how do we know that's gonna make her stop? Maybe she won't quit haunting us until we're dead," Bill said.

"That is a possibility, Mr. Barl—"

"Please, call me Bill," he interjected.

"Okay, *Bill*, that's a possibility," Jared continued, "but I do feel she'd rather not have to do that. Tabitha has help from a demon, so I gotta warn you, it's going to be tough to get rid of both of them."

"Bill, I think for once we can both agree neither of us want to turn ourselves in. Yes, we did a pretty crappy thing back in 2012, but we have a daughter to look after."

"But what about her?" Jessica piped up. "She had ... *has* a daughter, too. Can you imagine how it feels for her to have everything taken away?"

"Wait, are you saying you want us to go to the cops and tell them what we did?" Bertha said, her voice raised in surprise. "If we do that, your dad and me will be put away for a long time. There'd be nobody here to look after you."

"So you wanna go ahead with plan B and banish them like we did Caleb?" Jessica replied.

Bill interjected. "Jared, on a scale of one to ten, how creepy is this gonna be exactly if we go with the second plan?"

Jared paused for a minute, exchanging a worried glance with Jessica. She nodded for him to tell the truth.

"Look, I'm not gonna lie, it's gonna be tough—and somebody could get hurt if it's not done right."

"Great, we're screwed either way," Bill sighed.

"This way we get to stay outta jail," Bertha reminded him.

"Yeah, I guess," Bill said.

"So is tomorrow morning okay to do the exorcism?" Jared asked.

All three Barlows looked at one another until Bill spoke.

"Yeah. It is. Can we do it sooner, though? Just to get it over with?"

"It's safer during the day," Jared replied. He finished his soda and stood up, putting the glass on the table. "So can we meet—"

His glass scraping across the table made Jared stop.

"Oh no, it's happening again." Jessica got up from her bed, retreating towards the door.

"Did that just ...?" Bill uttered, consternation creeping into his voice.

"Still think we're making it up?" Jessica said.

"Now's not the time, Jess," Bertha advised.

There was a collective gasp when the glass tilted on its side by itself.

"Okay, everyone stay calm," Jared warned. "They want us to be scared so they can feed off our fear."

"What do we do?" Bertha said, now joining her daughter in moving towards the door.

"Do you still have some salt and holy—"

Another wave of gasps and screams came when the glass launched at Jared, cutting him off. The object stopped in mid-air, an inch from his nose.

"Okay, all right. Take it easy, guys," Jared reminded them, now breathing heavily himself, trying hard not to run out of the room. "Don't be afraid."

The glass changed direction, now aimed at Jessica.

"No!" Bill screamed, pushing Jessica out of the way. He ducked as the glass flew over his head, smashing off the wall.

"Salt and holy water. *Now!*" Jared shouted.

"Here," Bertha replied, opening her bedside locker door. She took some out and gave them to him.

Two pictures that had been sitting on Jessica's locker floated a few inches above it.

Bertha and Jessica ran for the door, followed closely by Bill. A chair resting beside it suddenly shot up in front of them. Its two front legs were raised, as if someone was carrying it, forcing them back.

Jared unscrewed the cork off the bottle and began sprinkling holy water on the floating object. "In Jesus' name, I command you to stop!"

The chair fell down.

He shouted to Jessica: "Quick, spread salt underneath the door and on the windowsills. Say the protection prayer!"

She did as Jared instructed while he continued dousing the motel room and recited the Archangel Michael prayer along with her.

Jared felt a chill surge down his spine, and something grabbed his hood. He found himself being dragged across the floor. The bathroom door flung open and he was launched inside. Jared grunted as he landed hard.

"Ow ... that hurt." He noticed the other three staring at him in horror and shock. Jessica and Bertha were crying.

"Don't ... stop. Keep going," he said.

Jessica jumped back into action, pouring salt underneath the front door while keeping an eye on her friend.

Catching the sink, Jared hauled himself up, rubbing his left shoulder. *Gotta finish this, and fast—before they do anything else.*

Just as Jared started to open the door, something slammed it shut again, jamming his fingers. A sickening crack confirmed the breaking of his bones.

"Arrgghh! Help me!" He let out a slew of obscenities as pain racked his left hand.

"Hold on!" Bill shouldered the door a few times, to no effect. More pressure was applied to Jared's trapped fingers.

"In Jesus' name ... I command you ..." Jared didn't have to finish. Whatever was keeping him inside the bathroom relinquished its hold, and Bill was finally able to come in.

"Come on, we'll get you to the hospital," Bill said.

Jared cradled his hand as they walked out the door, and Jessica joined Bertha in Bertha's car as they drove out of the parking lot.

***

Jessica sat in the cafeteria, waiting for Bill to bring her a soda. Bertha was waiting for Jared's parents to arrive.

A large lump lodged itself in Jessica's throat. She felt guilty for Jared being in hospital, even though none of this was her fault.

Bill returned to the table, placing a can in front of her.

"Oh, I know that look," he said. "Don't feel ashamed about Jared. If anything, it's your mother and mine's faults. He was just helping you out."

"Thanks ... but after the well, I *knew* doing this stuff was dangerous," Jessica replied.

"Jared feels that this is his calling. Maybe doing it gives him a sense of purpose."

Jessica pulled the ring back on the can. A hiss and a small

plume of fizz rose to greet her. "Still doesn't make me feel better."

An awkward silence fell between them, for a moment, until Bill broke it. "So … now that we're finally alone, is there anything you want to ask me or talk about?"

All this time, a million questions had piled up in Jessica's mind, each pushing forward and begging to be asked. A year, or even a week ago, she would've given anything for this opportunity to talk to her father. Now that he was here, she didn't know what to say except: "What did you do all this time?"

"Moved around a lot, going from job to job. I was working in a hardware store before your mom asked me to come here."

"Did you ever think of calling me?" Jessica asked.

"Every day, but like I said—"

"Yeah, I know, I know, Mom asked you not to. Still, you could've at least tried to reach out."

"Jess … when your mom found me in that hotel room with that waitress, I felt so ashamed. I was in a bad place—"

Jessica rolled her eyes.

"Look, I'm not making any excuses—"

"Sure sounds like it to me," Jessica butted in.

Bill paused, trying to remain calm. "Living with your mother after the accident wasn't easy. She was on my case about everything. If I left a sock on the floor, she'd nag about that. If I was home a few minutes late from work, she'd badger me about that too, asking forty questions."

Hearing this brought back memories of when Bertha was struggling with her drinking. Jessica would get the same treatment.

"I guess I can relate." She took a sip from the can, getting herself ready to ask something else. "So, what did you say in those letters?"

"I just wrote about how I missed you: missed those days going to the park, watching you play on the swings." He chuckled. "I missed movie nights and how you'd curl up beside me if we watched a horror movie. Looking back, we really shouldn't have let you see them."

"Yeah. I couldn't sleep for a few nights afterwards."

Bill kept the smile as he remembered. "Oh, that's right. You'd come running into our room wanting to sleep with us." He stroked the rim of his coffee cup. "Those were good times. Now that I'm back, maybe I could stay here and ... get to know you again?"

"It's going to take more than a soda to make things all right between us, Dad."

"I know, but I'd like a chance to do that. Can you give me one?"

More than anything else in the world, Jessica wanted her father to come back; but she felt conflicted. Part of her wanted to give him another chance, while another piece of her was afraid of being hurt again. Staring into his amber eyes brought back memories of him kissing her goodnight as a child.

"Okay, I'd like that. But it's going to take time," Jessica said.

"Sure. I understand."

***

The first rays of sunshine, ushering in a new day, shone on Jared's face, waking him up. Next came the pain in his fingers. He had been released from hospital last night, and he welcomed the sight of his own bed. The painkillers made him drowsy, so he'd slept longer than usual; and the heavy cast on his hand made his skin itchy.

Two knocks rapped on his door, and Maria stuck her head in. "Hey, baby. How are you this morning?"

"Sore, but I'll be fine. Don't worry."

Maria entered, shutting the door behind her. She pulled up a chair, sitting by his bedside. "Honey, we need to talk about ... your *calling*."

Jared gave her a weary glance. "Do we have to do this now, Ma?"

"It's something you need to think about. Jared, you could be killed next time!"

He winced while sitting up. "That's not gonna happen. Aunt Belle taught me how to protect myself."

"And look what good it did."

Jared knew she was right, but he was not going to give up on helping Jessica just yet. "If you're asking me to stop doing this, then the answer is no. Not while Jess needs my help."

Maria sat back, letting out a sigh of frustration. Her eyebrows pulled close and down, creating a crease in her forehead. "I know you guys have been friends for a long time, and I get that you wanna help her—"

"It's more than that, Ma. Jess has been a rock for me. Like Adrian. I can't turn my back on her now."

"Fine, but promise me two things."

"Go on."

"One: you'll rest a few days before finishing this case. And two: when you're done, that's it. No more ghostbustin', helping spirits or whatever the hell it is you do."

"I'll have to think about it."

Maria stood up, putting back the chair. Her nostrils flared as she smoothed down her purple blouse. "I'm going to make breakfast. I'd advise you to rethink your answer while you're getting up." She left hurriedly, fury present in every step she took.

Lying was not something Jared wanted to do to his mother. But he knew that this gift would be with him his whole life, and there would be many cases after Jessica's. Maybelle had warned him that helping the dead was dangerous and not everything on the other side was good, and there was a possibility that demons would attack from time to time, too. A part of him wanted to quit after helping the Barlows, but that wasn't in his nature.

Deep down, Jared was afraid of this demon. If it could break his fingers, what would stop it from killing him outright? But Jessica was one of his closest friends; and although he was scared, even if it meant taking his last breath, he'd die trying to protect her.

Jared's phone, vibrating on his locker, brought him back to the present. He picked it up.

Speak of the devil, he thought.

There was part of a text from Jessica on the screen. He tapped the notification and read it.

Hey, just checking in. Hope you're okay. Really sorry about all this.

As he was typing his reply, some of the good times he'd shared with Adrian and Jessica came flooding back. This made Jared even more determined to get rid of Tabitha and the demon.

***

Frost lingered in the air as Jessica stood outside Jared's front door with a "Get Well Soon" card and a box of chocolates. Many times, he'd talked about eating them while watching horror movies—they were his ultimate pick-me-up food. She kept stomping her feet and shifting around as she waited for someone to answer.

Maria opened it after a few minutes. Her warm and friendly "Hello" quickly turned to a stern and unwelcoming "Oh, it's you."

Bertha had told Jessica about the stern words Maria had for her at the hospital, before she'd picked up Jared, so Jessica was prepared for a cold reception.

"Hi, Mrs. Duval. I just wanted to give this to Jared."

Maria swiped the card and gift from Jessica's hand. "I'll be sure to pass it along. Anything else?"

"Could I talk to him for a second?"

"No, he's still resting. Try later. Now, I'm busy, so please excuse me."

Maria was about to close the door when Jared ran down the stairs.

"Hold on," he called, "I wanna talk to her."

"Jared, honey, you should be resting. Go back to bed."

"I'll be fine. I can rest later."

"But—"

"Ma, I know you mean well; but please just stop, okay?" Jared grumbled. "I'm not a kid anymore."

Maria thrust the box of chocolates into his chest. "Fine. But the next time you get hurt helping *her*, she can look after you!"

Maria more stomped than walked away, head raised in the air.

With flushed cheeks, Jared avoided eye contact with Jessica for a few seconds until Maria had gone into kitchen. He was about to speak when his mother slammed the door.

"Look, sorry about my mom. She's just being overprotective."

"No need to apologize. It's me who should be saying sorry. You got hurt helping us, and we all feel really bad." Jessica paused. "Jared ... maybe you should sit this one out."

"What? No. Like I said to Ma yesterday, you and Adrian were there for me when I needed backup, what with Lydia and those other homophobes. It's gonna take more than a few broken fingers to stop me solving this. Besides"—he checked to see if the kitchen door was still closed, then continued in a low voice—"Aunt Belle always taught me to never give up."

"Still, I don't want you to end up with a broken leg or ... worse."

"Jess, I'm not quitting, so don't even try to talk me out of it."

"Okay."

He stepped back inside, waving at Jessica to enter. She stared at the kitchen, showing her reluctance.

"Hey, don't worry about her. She'll cool down," Jared said.

"All right."

They went into the living room.

"So, how are they?" Jessica asked him, nodding at the cast.

"Sore, but that's to be expected. How are things between you and your dad?"

"I don't know. The whole thing feels just ... weird, to be honest. He asked me to give him another chance."

"And ...?"

"I said I would. We're meeting at Jackie's in about twenty minutes."

"That's good, right? It shows he's tryin', and he did come when your mom asked him to."

"Yeah, I know, but there's eight *years* to make up for. It's gonna take a long while."

"At least he's taking the first step. How many folks out there would kill for an opportunity like this?"

Jessica nodded in agreement. Having this conversation solidified her belief that Bill being back in Hopps Town was an opportunity that should be grabbed with both hands.

"You're right, as always," she said. "Have you been catching up on Dr. Phil?"

"I was always smart and beautiful," Jared joked. They laughed, something Jessica hadn't done much of since this whole ordeal began.

"Good thing you still got your sense of humor." Jessica checked her watch. "Guess I better be going. Take it easy, and make sure you rest."

"I'll try, but—one last thing. Have you guys thought about getting a priest?"

"We already did, but Mom thinks it didn't work. He barely believed us before calling to the house. She's getting another one to come tonight."

"I hope it works."

"Me too. Look, I really gotta go. Text you later."

Jared walked her to the door. "Remember to stock up on holy water and pure salt. You know ... just in case."

"We will, don't worry. Bye, Jared."

***

Jessica sat in Jackie's enjoying a delicious strawberry-and-banana milkshake. Bill had arrived before her and ordered a burger and a soda. He wore a red scarf around his neck.

"What's with the scarf?" she asked.

"Damn cheap cologne. Bought it in a gift store. Put it on this morning and ten minutes later I'm breaking out in a rash. Never thought I'd be allergic to that."

They shared a laugh, breaking any awkwardness that hung in the air.

For two hours, Jessica talked to her dad about high school and college life. The usual question about boyfriends came up, and she blushed.

"No, Dad. Haven't been with anyone in a while. The last few years have been ... eventful."

"I bet, if they were anything like a few days ago."

She explained that they hadn't always been haunted by supernatural beings. For seven years, everything was pretty normal, despite Bertha's drinking and abusive behavior. On more than one occasion, Jessica hinted that Bill was the only thing missing from their lives.

"You know, Jess, there were so many times I wanted to just get in the car, drive out here and take you away," he said, "but I couldn't."

"Why not? I mean, everything could've changed if you had. Maybe you guys could've worked something out."

"It was more complicated than that. If I'd come back into your life while you were still in high school, it could've interfered with your studying. It just would've been ... hard for everyone. But you gotta believe me, I really did want to come and whisk you away." Bill raised his glass. "Can I get another soda, please?"

Directing his attention to Jessica again, he said, "I have to go to the little boys' room. Back in a jiffy."

Bill was about to get up when he noticed Jessica's face grow ashen.

"What's wrong?" he asked.

"I think there's a cop coming towards us."

"Oh, great," Bill mumbled.

A tall man with a skin-tight haircut stopped at their table. "Excuse me, are you Mr. Barlow?"

"Yes."

The man flashed his badge. "Detective Ramirez, HT PD." He put the badge back into his pocket. "Do you mind if I have a word with you outside?"

"Well, I'm actually just having lunch with my daughter, here."

"I understand that, sir. It won't take a minute."

"How about later?"

"Or we could go down to the station to do this. Your call," Detective Ramirez said.

Bill sighed, wiping his mouth with a napkin, and stood up. "Okay, let's go outside."

Detective Ramirez held the door open for Bill, who followed him. "I was speaking to your wife a few days ago," he said. "I got a few questions about August 12th, 2012."

"What about it?" Bill asked, sticking his hands into his pockets.

"Can you tell me where you were that night?"

"Gosh, that's eight years ago. Hard to remember that far back."

"Can you please try?"

Bill lowered his head in thought for a moment. "August 12th?"

The detective nodded.

"Wait ... I think I remember now. Oh yeah, I was watching our daughter while my ex-wife went to her mother's house."

"Anything happen on the way back?"

Bill had been prepared for this. Bertha had told him about the detective's questions, and they'd gone over their story. "Um ... I think she hit a deer."

"And can you tell me what car she was driving?"

"A silver Sedan, I think."

"Was it a 2005 model?"

"Yeah, think so. Sorry, Detective, why are you asking me all these questions?"

"I'm following up on some leads for the Tabitha Logan case. So, how long are you back in Hopps Town?"

"A few days. Just came by to visit my daughter."

Detective Ramirez regarded him with a suspicious gaze. "The same daughter you haven't seen in eight years?"

"Yeah. Again, where are you going with this?" Bill pressed, a little firmer.

"The timing is pretty coincidental, don't you think? I mean, you've been gone since 2012. Then we find Mrs. Logan's body, and suddenly you're back in town. Anything you wanna tell us?"

"Nope. I've told you everything I know."

"Lying to a police officer is a chargeable offence," Detective

Ramirez reminded him. "You are aware of that, right?"

"Yes, sir, I am."

The detective's eyes studied Bill's posture and reaction. Bill remained still and calm despite his heart hammering against the chest.

Detective Ramirez handed him a card. "That's my number. If you think of anything else, give me a call—and don't leave town anytime soon."

Bill looked at the card as the detective walked away.

Let's hope we can end this without somebody dying or going to jail.

He went inside to the bathroom.

Bill rinsed his hands and dried them. Everything had gone smoothly today, even better than he expected. Being able to sit down with Jessica was a dream he'd had since leaving eight years ago. Bill thought that maybe he might get to see her at her wedding if he was lucky. Never had he dreamed that it would be much sooner, and under these circumstances.

I'm just really glad she's back in my life, Bill thought.

The main door opened, and Bill moved over to avoid being hit. It stayed open for what felt like half a minute, but nobody came in.

What the heck?

With both hands still dripping wet, Bill walked around and looked in both directions. There was nobody about.

Oh no, it's happening again, he thought, retreating back into the toilets. He snapped off a few pieces of tissue.

Just as Bill was about to leave, something snagged on his scarf. He spun around, eyes scanning every inch of the room to see who had pulled at it. A foul smell of rotten food infiltrated his nose, and a frosty cold descended on him. He could see his breath.

The door slamming shut behind him confirmed the tingling feeling in his spine. Bill was most definitely not alone.

Children's laughter surrounded him, reverberating off the walls. Soon, it transformed into maniacal, evil cackling.

"I don't know what you want, but please leave me alone," he

begged.

"You know what we want," a voice replied, echoing in Bill's mind.

"We already apologized. We have a daughter, and—"

"No more excuses," the voice butted in. "Time to pay the piper!"

Bill suddenly found himself facing the wall, pinned up against it. His scarf was pulled hard, slowly tightening around his neck. Bill grabbed it, trying to prize it off him.

Stars and black dots appeared in the corner of his sight. The hold was getting stronger, choking the life from him. He tried to scream, but couldn't get enough air to even yelp.

A glossy magazine rested on the table beside Jessica. She picked it up and browsed through some articles while waiting for Bill to return.

A fluttering feeling in her stomach and dizziness hit simultaneously. Her head arched back, and her green eyes were covered in a luminous white hue.

What's happening to me? she thought.

Images of Bill fighting for his life, trying to free himself from some invisible attacker yanking his scarf, now played out before her. His eyes bulged as he clawed the air in a failed attempt to break free.

The white light vanished, as did the strange sensations.

"What the hell ...?" Jessica muttered before leaping out of her seat, running to the men's room.

As she tried to open the door, a powerful force kept it closed. She could hear her father moving around frantically.

What would Jared do now? Jessica thought. She remembered that he'd made the sign of the Cross back in the motel and commanded the entity to stop.

That's it.

Crossing herself, Jessica shouted, "I command you, in Jesus' name, to open this door and leave my dad alone!" Once more, Jessica shouldered the door, almost falling into the room when nothing tried to stop her. She caught the sink to prevent herself from stumbling.

Bill's face was red and he was breathing heavily. Jessica helped him unwrap the scarf, which had left an abrasion as a reminder of the attack.

"Oh, thank God ... you're here," Bill said, his voice a little hoarse.

Guess we got to get Jared after all. I better call Mom and warn her, Jessica thought as she helped her dad back to the booth.

***

11.30 a.m. was Bertha's favorite time in the morning. This marked the start of a fifteen-minute break; and to her, there was nothing sweeter than lying back in her office chair and sipping a hot espresso. Lately, she hadn't been resting much, what with Tabitha and the demon pursuing her family.

When Jared was put out of action, she'd contacted the local priest that same day. Bertha couldn't give the whole story, but she did tell him that they were being haunted by a nasty entity. Bertha asked if he could come and bless their motel room and house. She remembered hearing the dread in the man's voice as he slowly agreed to do it.

A day later, he came and performed the blessing, but the comforting feeling she had expected never came. She hoped the second priest would be more effective.

Bertha stretched her arms. She'd gotten a text from Jessica a few minutes ago, but hadn't read it yet.

I'll do that once my break is over, she thought, relishing a moment's peace and quiet.

On the desk was a picture of herself and her daughter, taken at Christmas when Jessica was home for the holidays. They both wore Santa hats. Behind them was a tree bedecked in green, red and blue tinsel. Twinkling fairy lights gave the tree an almost ethereal glow. Every time Bertha looked at that photo, it made her smile, brightening up her day.

"I'm lucky to have you, Jess," Bertha said, stroking the picture. "And I'll be damned if I'm gonna let some ghost destroy our happiness."

A glance at the clock showed that her break was over. Another thought came into her head.

"Oh, that's right," she said to herself. "Got to bless the office again."

Jared had advised her to do that every couple of hours, just for added protection.

Bertha pulled open a drawer in the desk. She was about to take out the bottle of holy water when her phone rang. She answered.

"Hey, Jess, honey. I didn't get—"

"Mom, you need to listen to me," Jessica said, her words crashing into one another in panic.

"Whoa, hold on. Is everything okay?"

"Dad ... he was attacked ..."

"Attacked? How?"

"Meet me—" Static filled the line, blocking out what Jessica was saying.

"Jess, I can't hear you! What was that?"

"You need .... to ... out ... there!" Once more, static infiltrated the line.

"I can't hear what you're saying!"

The line went dead.

Jumping into action, Bertha grabbed the holy water. Just as she was about to sprinkle it, something knocked the bottle out of her hand. Bertha leapt back in fright.

"Oh, crap!" she yelled, her heart beating faster than ever before.

Scurrying and scratching on the walls made her retreat slowly. It sounded like hundreds of vermin were around her, yet there were no creatures. The noises persisted, forcing Bertha to flee.

As she got to the door, it burst open, hitting her face. Bertha fell back and struck the table, knocking the picture of her and Jessica to the floor and shattering the glass.

"Damn it!"

Bertha got up, ready to race out of the room, when the door slammed shut. She was trapped with whatever was here.

Her shock turned to dismay as a shard of glass floated a few inches off the ground, aimed directly at her.

"Oh, please, don't hurt me …" Bertha pleaded.

The daylight coming in from the window was blocked when one of the shutter cords was pulled, bringing it down. Her office grew darker, each shutter closing one by one.

Bertha fumbled around for the light switch. When she found it and pressed it, the bulb blew.

"God, no," she shrieked, her hands trembling.

The shard of glass, now floating higher than before, reflected what little light that found its way in. Bertha jumped again when the office swelled with a chorus of whispering voices.

"Stop it! Please stop!" Bertha cried, covering her ears and falling to her knees. "Somebody help me!"

One voice rose above the multitude. "Time ... to pay ... the piper ... bitch," the demon said.

The shard of glass zipped toward Bertha, too fast to avoid. She screamed as it thrust into her left arm and blood soaked her white blouse.

"Please ... I'll turn ... myself … in!" Bertha yelled in agony as the glass twisted ninety degrees clockwise, deepening the wound.

"Time's ... up," snarled the demon.

Bertha's eyes bulged with fright as another piece of glass hovered, turning towards her. "No ... please, *no!*"

The door opened. Norman was about to speak, but was rendered speechless by what he saw. The glass shot at Bertha, this time missing her left ear by an inch and embedding itself into the wall.

"Sweet Jesus," Norman exclaimed.

"Norman, help me ... dammit!" Bertha shouted, snapping him out of his trance.

Norman caught her right arm, pulling Bertha up. "Come on. I'll get you out of here."

They half-walked, half-ran out of her office, leaving a trail of blood from each drop that fell from the wound.

***

The time on Maybelle's phone read *11:50*. Boredom had set in a few hours ago. There was only so much reading and scrolling a person could do. Maybelle was tired of being in hospital and wished she was at home. Staring up at the ceiling and four walls, eating crappy food and meeting some nurses who were sadly lacking a bedside manner had taken its toll on her, making her more antsy than normal.

"Think happy thoughts, girl, think happy thoughts" was a mantra Maybelle had developed since she was admitted into hospital, but even the effectiveness of that was waning.

First thing I'm gonna do when I'm outta here is have a bath.

Another thing that was on her mind was Jared. Yesterday, Oscar let her know through a text message that he broke three fingers while helping his friend. She knew Maria was angry and probably blamed her for him being involved in all this. It would make Maybelle curse sometimes when she'd imagine Maria nagging Jared about using his God-given gift to help others. Hyacinth, Maybelle and Oscar's mother, never did that, because she had the gift, too. She always encouraged her children to use it, but always reminded them to be careful.

Just as Maybelle was drifting off to sleep, a smell of roses invaded the room. To her, this meant only one thing: a vision.

"Oh no, I hate—"

She didn't have time to finish that sentence when her upper torso arched and her eyes rolled back into their sockets.

She was in a forest, but everything was in black and white. She sensed a sinister force lurking about, flitting from tree to tree. Shouting from behind made her turn around. There, she saw Jessica running with a man; and, in the distance, she heard Jared calling after them.

In a blink, Maybelle was at Jared's location, watching him dash toward his friend. A black shadow jumped down behind him, racing towards the boy.

As Jared ran, he looked over his shoulder every couple of seconds, seeing the creature gain on him. It reached out a tentacle, grabbing his maroon-colored hoodie. With great force, it yanked at it, pulling him to the ground.

"No!" Maybelle screamed.

Jared didn't get up as the shadow raced past him, heading for Jessica.

The vision ended. Maybelle was back in the hospital room, sweat breaking out on her forehead.

"I gotta warn J ..."

As Maybelle dialed his number, she saw that—as she'd come to expect from the hospital ward—there was no signal on her phone.

Damn. What am I gonna do now?

The help button hanging beside her bed gave Maybelle an idea. She pressed it.

Just hope they don't think I'm crazy asking for a phone, she thought. Maybelle hoped even more that it wouldn't be too late to tell Jared not to go to the forest.

*** * ****

Bill held Jessica's hand as they sat in the waiting room. After leaving the café, Norman phoned to let her know that Bertha had been rushed to hospital. The doctors told them that she was being treated for a deep stab wound on her arm, and also for shock.

Jessica had felt sorry for Norman as he stuttered on the phone, still trying to make sense of what he saw. She knew that the demon struck again.

This was the final straw.

"What next?" she asked, struggling to hold back the tears. "*Who's* next? Me? You?"

"Calm down, Jess."

"Mom's been stabbed by a ..." She stopped, lowering her voice. "By a friggin' demon, and you want me to *calm down?*"

"I know you're upset and worried," Bill said. "So am I, but getting worked up about it won't help anyone."

"We gotta do something, Dad, before someone gets killed."

"What about the priest? Maybe if we—"

"The first priest didn't work. What makes you think the second one will?" Jessica said.

"Maria's angry at us. She's not going to let Jared help."

"He said he would, no matter how she felt."

"Will the poor kid be able to? His hand's in a cast," Bill said with a great deal of doubt.

This was something Jessica continued to feel guilty over; and, now, that they needed Jared more than ever, she felt it a lot more. She hated the idea of possibly causing him further pain.

"I don't know. But after we see Mom, I'm gonna call him," she said.

Jessica could tell by Bill's posture and face that there was something he wanted to say but wasn't. "Come on, out with it."

"This thing won't stop until we either turn ourselves in or are dead. I feel like there's not enough time for Jared to do his thing."

"What are you trying to say?"

"Maybe it might be best if I hand myself over to the cops."

Jessica stood up, eyeing him in shock. "No! You've been gone for eight years, and you want to do *this?*"

"Jess, sit down, please." She did so with reluctance. "You guys are important to me. If anything happened, I'd never forgive myself. Besides, you managed without me for the last eight years."

"No, we didn't. Mom was a mess. I was in hell living with her until she stopped drinking. Every day I wished you were in my life, and now that I have that, you wanna take it away!"

"There's no choice. It's getting worse," Bill said, raising his voice more than he intended. He paused, taking a deep breath, before speaking more calmly. "Something needs to be done, because the more we sit around and talk this over, more bad things are gonna happen. It has to be me, Jess. You need your mom."

"No, look—just give me twenty four hours to come up with something. If I don't have anything by then, fine, we'll do it your way."

"The longer we sit around here thinking, the higher the chance of another attack. We gotta make the first strike this time." Bill massaged his furrowed brows. There were dark circles around his eyes. "I gotta get a coffee. Want a soda, candy?"

"No, I'm good."

"Okay. Stay here and I won't be long." Bill left.

A tall East-Asian doctor entered the waiting room. He pushed up his blue-rimmed glasses while approaching Jessica with a clipboard in his hand.

"Are you Mrs. Barlow's daughter?" he asked.

"Yes."

"You can see her now, if you wish. She's a little out of it. We had to give her morphine to ease the pain and a sedative to calm her down. She'll need some counselling; the attack was traumatizing for her."

You don't know the half of it, Jessica thought. "Okay, thanks."

"Try to keep it short. She'll be lucid only for a few minutes at a time."

"Got it."

Jessica walked down the hall and entered the room where Bertha lay. Her mother stared out the window, her eyes red from crying.

"Mom," Jessica said, half-running to hug her.

"Whoa, easy, honey," Bertha replied, gently keeping her daughter back. "My arm's still pretty sore, although the meds are kicking in now."

Jessica pulled up a chair to sit beside the bed. "So, what exactly happened? Norman said you were attacked."

"I was. That damn demon came at me again. Thought I was gonna die."

"Dad and I were talking about this and ... well, he wants to turn himself in."

"What? No ... he can't."

101

"He seems determined. We gotta do the exorcism—it's the only way to end this and stop Dad from ending up behind bars. I just hope Jared will be up for it."

"Maria's gonna try and persuade him not to. Can't say I blame her. Poor kid broke his fingers trying to protect us," Bertha said.

The crucifix hanging on the wall opposite Bertha's bed gave Jessica an idea.

"Maybe I should phone Jared now." She checked Bertha's water jug, saw that it was empty. "Do you want a drink?"

"No ... I'm good. Feeling a little tired."

"I'll be back later." Jessica kissed her mother's forehead before leaving.

Once outside, Jessica phoned her friend.

"Hi. Do you still have that special crucifix?"

"Uh-huh," Jared said. "Sure. Why?"

"My mom's gonna need it. There's been another incident. Can I come over?"

"Like, right now?" Jared asked.

"Yeah. I know it's kind of late, but we need your help ... like, really badly," Jessica replied.

"Okay. Might be best to park down the street. Mom's still mad."

"Kinda figured that. See you in twenty minutes."

***

Jared wiped down the small gold crucifix with a cloth before stuffing it inside his jacket. He knew things must have gotten a whole lot worse if Jessica was asking for this.

Don't worry, Jess, I'm gonna do everything I can to protect you, Jared thought.

He waited until Maria had gone into the living room to watch TV. When she closed the door, Jared knew it was time to make his escape.

Creeping down the stairs, Jared was filled with relief when he left the house undetected. In a semi-hunched stance, he sprinted to

Jessica's car, which was parked four houses down from his own.

"Wassup?" he said, getting in.

"Thanks for meeting me," she said. "Have you got it?"

"The crucifix? Sure." Jared took out the beautiful, polished object. "How bad is it with your mom?"

"The demon stabbed her. Could've been a lot worse, but ..."

"Oh, crap. Sorry to hear that, Jess."

Jessica took the crucifix from him, marveling at the intricate detail. "Wow, this is really neat. And you said this is blessed, right?"

"Yeah. Aunt Belle told me that a priest got it blessed by the Virgin Mary in some place in Croatia. Can't remember the name."

"Just hope this protects my mom. I appreciate you giving it to me," Jessica said.

"Like I said before, any time."

Jessica opened the glove compartment, rummaging around for something to hold the crucifix. She found a folded-up, black paper bag, slid it inside, and tied the bag shut.

"Jared, there's something else I wanna talk about. We need to end this ... like, right now. I'm so worried about my parents. Dad wants to turn himself in. I can't ..." Jessica stopped for a moment. A quiver crept into her words, and she took a deep breath. Jared saw her trying to fight back tears.

"I can't lose my dad again." She gazed at him with pleading eyes. "Please, Jared, we have to do the exorcism tomorrow. This *has* to end. Do you think you'll be able to?"

"Gotta admit, it could be tough with one hand, but I'll try."

"We'll be there to help, too. You won't be alone."

"Thanks. Get that cross to your mom ASAP, okay? We'll meet first thing tomorrow morning."

"I'll be here bright and early." Jessica held up a clenched fist. Jared bumped it.

"Better get back before Mom notices I'm gone."

Jared got out. Just as he was about to close the door, Jessica added, "Thanks again. This means a lot."

"No problem." Jared winked.

While running back, he kept low, trying to hide underneath the bushes as he moved along them.

Tomorrow's gonna be hard, but it's what I'm here to do. I'm scared, but I can't let Jessica or her family down, Jared thought as he snuck past the living room and climbed back up to bed, careful not to make any noise.

***

Malik stood by the masonry fireplace, feeling the flames' warmth on his skin. His eyes were closed and he zoned in on Tabitha's location. This was a trick he'd learned right after his fall from Heaven for joining Lucifer's army. Once their leader had turned against humans, fallen angels gained new skills and abilities to lure mankind away from God.

Malik found Tabitha. She was hovering around Jessica and Bertha's hotel room, about to make her way to the hospital. Their reign of terror was working, and he loved toying with the Barlows.

A slight whooshing sound disturbed his meditation. He was no longer alone. A powerful presence had entered the abyss.

It was Satan.

Malik genuflected and bowed his head. "My Lord," he greeted. "We've made progress."

"Apart from maiming the mother, all three of those humans are still alive! How can you call that *progress?*"

"I know, my lord. I am working towards that."

"Work faster! Enough mind games. End this *now*."

"Yes, Your Majesty."

With that, the King of Hell vanished.

***

Never in his nineteen years on Earth had Jared felt as tense as he did now. His shoulders were rigid, heavy with the burden of what had to be done. He swallowed a large lump of dread lodged in his throat, keeping up a brave façade, hiding his consternation with small smiles.

Today it literally was all or nothing for him, Jessica and her family. Three people relied on Jared carrying out the exorcism successfully. His earlier doubts, wondering if he was good or powerful enough to do this, started to invade his mind.

During the night, Jared got up and said a prayer, hoping to stop them.

God, help me today. I'm scared, man, Jared thought.

Resting beside his right leg was a rucksack containing pure salt, holy water and a spare blessed crucifix Maybelle had given him. Jared wondered what his aunt would say if she were here now.

I miss her pep talks. She'd probably say something like, "Don't give into negative thinking, J. You got this."

Gazing up at the ceiling, he added in a low voice, "Grandma, if you're listening, can you put in a good word to the Big Man, or even help me today? I need it."

His phone dinged, interrupting his prayer. It was a text from Jessica.

I'm outside.

"Guess it's showtime," Jared mumbled. He grabbed his bag and once more, navigated the stairs as if he were a thief making a sneaky exit. Maria was at work, so he only had to get past Oscar. Craning his neck to peek into the living room, Jared couldn't see his dad. A feeling of relief swept through his body as he quietly stepped out the door.

Phew, that was clo—

"Where ya goin', son?" Oscar asked.

I spoke too soon.

Jared turned around to face his father. "Just heading out, Dad."

Oscar, with his arms folded, stood by the side of their house, leaning up against the wall. "You wouldn't happen to be going ghostbustin' with Jessica, would ya?"

"Nah, I'm just—"

"What did I say about lying?" Oscar said in a firm tone. His eyes narrowed, fixing a stern gaze on his son.

Jared's shoulders slouched and he lowered his head. "All right, you got me. Yeah, I'm going to help them. They need it, Dad."

"And you're going to do that with just one arm? I thought you knew better than that." Oscar walked to where Jared was, meeting his son's browbeaten stare. "You're going up against something evil. I know it's not your first rodeo; but they have the advantage already, and it ain't even started yet."

"Talking about my hand?" Jared asked.

"Ding ding, we have a winner! Yes, your hand."

"Jessica said she'd help out, so I'll be fine."

"No. I'm going with you," Oscar insisted.

"Sorry, Dad, no offence … but you'll only get in the way."

"How?"

"Because they could attack you, and that'll mean rescuing another person."

Oscar folded his toned arms again. The unimpressed expression returned. "So I'm supposed to just wait here until it's done and not protect my own son? Is that what I'm hearing?"

"Aunt Maybelle taught me well. You're just going to have to trust me, and God, that I'll come home okay."

"That's a big ask. I wouldn't let any of my troops go out on their own on a suicide mission. I'd be front and center," Oscar said.

"This isn't a suicide mission, Dad," Jared scoffed.

"Could've fooled me. Oh, and I saw you sneak out last night, too."

Panic washed over Jared's face.

"Uh-huh. Didn't think I'd see that, huh?" Oscar continued.

"Does Mom know?"

Oscar shook his head. "She should, though. Don't like keeping secrets from her."

"Dad, this is important to me. Jess's mom is in the hospital. Jess and her dad could be attacked at any moment. I'm the only one who can stop that from happening. She means a lot to me, Pop. I can't let her down. Would you let any of your men down?"

Oscar shifted, presenting his son with a softer gaze this time. "No, I wouldn't." Oscar sighed. "All right, here's the deal. I'm gonna give you two hours to get this done. Got it?"

"Sure. Thanks, Dad."

"Give me your phone."

"Why?" Jared asked with an arched eyebrow.

Oscar beckoned for the cell, and Jared gave it to him. Oscar navigated to the Settings screen, tapping the button to turn on the location finder.

"Do *not* turn that off. If I don't hear from you in two hours, I'm coming."

"Thanks. Don't worry, everything'll be fine." Jared took back the cell.

"Better be. By the way, your aunt phoned last night and said to watch your back when doing the exorcism. She thinks something might attack you from behind. She tried to call you but your phone was turned off."

"Okay. Thanks for the warning."

"Thank her when it's over," Oscar said.

Jared picked up his bag and walked off before Oscar changed his mind.

"Be careful, son," Oscar called out.

"I will be."

God, don't let me down, man.

Jared got into Jessica's car.

"Let's go. Can we make a quick stop at St. Peter's first?" he said.

"Sure. Can I ask why?"

"I'll explain on the way."

He hoped that the new priest, Father Dominic, was hearing confessions. Maybelle told him once that for an exorcism to work, a person must be free from sin. There was no better way to get that than absolution.

***

The forest was serene. Clear blue skies, and an aroma of sap from the trees, put everyone at ease as Jared finished pouring salt for a circle of protection. Jessica and Bill stood inside it.

Thank God Father Dominic heard my confession. I just want to get this over with, Jared thought, covering the can of pure salt and stepping inside the circle.

"What now?" Jessica asked.

"We call for Tabitha," Jared replied.

"Do you think she'll come?" Bill said, scanning their surroundings.

"I think so. Like I said back in the car: no matter what happens, stay inside the circle. This will protect us, all right?"

Both Barlows nodded.

Jared swept the trees with his own eyes, yelling, "Yo, Tabitha Logan! I call on the spirit of Tabitha Logan!"

There was a shift in the atmosphere as a small breeze laced with a cold tinge blew around them.

"Is she here?" Jessica said, glancing left and right.

"Not yet," Jared replied, "but close. Tabitha Logan, I summon you!"

Jared felt a chill sensation circling the nape of his neck. He spun around. Standing a few inches away from the them all was Tabitha, glaring at Bill.

"She's here," Jared announced, directing his attention at her. "Look, Tabitha—can I call you that?"

She nodded, her focus never leaving Bill.

"Thank you. We've come to end this. I—" Jared continued.

"Is he turning himself in?" Tabitha interrupted.

"Tabitha, we just—"

"Is. He. Turning. Himself. In?"

"Maybe we can work something out?" Jared countered.

"That doesn't answer my question," she bellowed, her roar disturbing leaves in the trees and knocking them off their branches. Bill and Jessica jumped.

"Relax. We just want to talk, that's all." Jared spoke calmly, trying to maintain control.

"The time for talking is over. I want to know right now: is he or Bertha, going to confess to the cops?" Impatience infiltrated Tabitha's tone.

108

"I know what they did was wrong. Heck, they know that too, and they feel bad about it."

"So that's a no?" Tabitha said, her voice a few octaves higher, both fists balled.

Uh-oh, gotta do something before it gets outta hand. "I'm not saying that."

"Then what are you trying to say?"

"What's she talking about?" Jessica asked, standing close to her father. Bill put a protective arm around her.

"She wants to know if your mom or dad will turn themselves in," Jared said.

Bill spoke just as Jessica was about to. "If that's what it means to end this, then fine, I'll do it. Just don't hurt my daughter, or Bertha."

"Dad, wait, we came—"

"No, Jess, this has gone on long enough," Bill said, cutting her off. "I don't want somebody else to pay the price for what we did."

Jessica shrugged off Bill's arm, stepping close to the circle's edge. "Is she here?" she asked, pointing to a spot in front of her.

"Yeah, but stay inside," Jared warned.

"I will. Tabitha, I know what my parents did was wrong, and we do want to make things right. I know you never got a chance to spend much time with your daughter—"

Jared cut her off. "Easy, Jess."

"The thing is, I missed out on eight years of having my dad around. He felt so bad about what happened that he left Hopps Town. Now that he's back, I can't lose him again. Please don't take him away."

"Fine, but tell them Bertha's gotta hand herself over. Otherwise ..." Tabitha warned.

Jared gulped, knowing exactly what the ghost meant. "Um ... she said okay, but your mom's got to take your dad's place. Someone has to go to jail. I know it's not what you guys want but .. .you know..."

"Then it has to be me," Bill stated.

"Wait, Dad, can't we—"

"No, I'm not taking any chances." He turned to where he thought Tabitha was standing. "Okay, you win. But I just wanna say something, first. What Jess said earlier, about us being sorry for what we did, is true."

Jared could see anguish on the man's face.

Bill carried on as Jessica started sobbing. "We really are, and I'm going to make things right. I want assurances, though. When I walk into that police station and confess, will you leave them alone?" Bill asked.

"If he does, then yes," Tabitha said in stern tone.

"She said you've a deal," Jared said.

Blood drained from Jared's face, and he broke out in a cold sweat as the chill wind became biting, almost as if snow was about to fall. Everyone could see their breath now. He knew this meant one thing: they had company. The kind nobody wanted.

"NO!" the demon boomed, his cry reverberating around the forest.

"What's wrong?" Jessica said as Bill pulled her behind him.

"W—We got more company," Jared revealed, trying with all his might to conceal the trepidation filling every pore in his body.

The demon swirled into view as a cloud of black, menacing smoke, then took the form of the tall, suave, handsome man.

The icy breeze now became a strong gale.

"We had a deal, Peaches," the demon growled. "They were to *suffer.*"

"And they have, Malik, but I've gotten what I wanted: justice."

"Justice?" Malik scoffed. "Do you really think when he leaves here that he'll keep his word?"

"What's going on, Jared?" Jessica shouted.

"Just a second, Jess. Mr. Barlow, are you really going to the police after we're done here?" Jared asked.

"Yes, on my kid's life," Bill replied.

"There, you see. It's over," Tabitha said.

"Over? Not even close. I don't want them to just suffer. They must *die!*" Malik eyes glowed blood-red as he reached out his left hand, moving it upwards, as if beckoning something.

All inside the circle took a few steps back as stones rose up around them

"M—Mother of G—God," Bill stuttered.

Jared gulped, again putting on a brave voice. "Everybody chill. I know this looks bad, but stay where you are."

Malik cast his hand forward. Stones pelted the invisible wall.

"Christ!" Bill screamed, causing Jessica to jump.

"Your little circle won't keep you safe for much longer."

The demon motioned for more stones to rise. They levitated, hanging in the air, aiming for the three frightened humans.

"Stop. He's turning himself in. That's enough," Tabitha pleaded.

"I'll say when it's *enough*. And as for you, be gone." Malik slapped her hard with the back of his right hand, sending Tabitha crashing into a nearby tree. She didn't get up.

"I can't stand weakness," Malik added.

Again the little missiles pelted and bounced off the holy forcefield.

Bill fell back, his face completely ashen.

"Screw this."

He got up and fled.

"Dad, wait!" Jessica called.

"Don't," Jared said, noticing that her expression had shifted from inner conflict to dread. Jessica stared at the circle of salt and then at her father.

She chased after him.

"Jess, no!" Jared shouted.

Malik laughed, his guffaws rumbling like thunder. "Run, little piggies. *Run!*" He disappeared, beginning the hunt for his prey.

"Dang it," Jared cursed, also leaving the safety of the circle.

The farther Jared ran into the forest, the more Maybelle's warning preyed on his mind. Every ten seconds or so he'd look back, making sure Malik wasn't behind him. But he could see the demon in his peripheral vision, appearing and disappearing behind the trees.

Jessica and her father were fast runners, and, being an arm

111

down, Jared found it hard to keep up while trying not to fall over logs and large stones that were hidden under leaves or covered over by bushes.

"Yo, Jess! Mr. Barlow! Wait up. Come back!"

"Jared!" Jessica cried out, but she didn't stop to wait for him.

"It's no use, boy. They're lost to you now. Give up," Malik taunted him telepathically.

"Keep away, man," Jared yelled.

The sounds of the forest became amplified, every flapping of a birds' wings or creaking of branches being twice as loud. The foliage became dense, closing in on all sides.

"I told you ..." Malik said. This time, his words echoed around Jared in a singsong tone. "They're mine."

The last two words came from right behind the boy. It was too late for him to turn around and defend himself.

A large hand caught his hoodie, hurling him against a rough tree trunk. Jared's back and head hit it, hard. Darkness engulfed him.

When Jared awoke, he was in a familiar-looking kitchen. Sunflower wallpaper, the sweet smell of home-baked apple pie, pictures of his cousins on the windowsill and the sign made out of clay that read *A Woman's Castle is Her Home* ... this place could belong to only one person: Grandma Hyacinth.

What the hell am I doing here?

"Hello," Jared called out. "Am I dead?"

An unexpected, gentle laugh should have made him jump; but instead, it put him at ease, slowing his thundering heart.

"No, child. You're not dead."

Hyacinth, with open arms, walked into the kitchen, giving her grandson a tight hug. "Good to see you again, Jared."

Jared didn't reciprocate the embrace, keeping his free hand to the side and standing there in shock. "What's happening, Grandma?"

"That big old demon knocked you out, but God has given us a minute to talk."

"So I'm definitely not dead?"

Hyacinth shook her head.

"Phew. I'm glad about that." Jared wiped his brow.

"We don't have much time, so I wanna say somethin'." She gave him one of those playful, semi-stern looks. "So shut your pie-hole and open up these." Hyacinth tugged on his ears.

"What is it?"

"I know you're doubting yourself about beating Mr. Nasty out there. Yes, he's strong—but so are you," Hyacinth said.

"Am I really, Grandma? This isn't like the one we faced at the well a year ago. He's stronger, faster, meaner. He broke my fingers. How can I beat something like that?"

"The same way you beat the last one: with faith and inner strength. God never gives us something we can't handle. How many times did I tell you that?"

"Too many," Jared replied.

"And I was right, wasn't I?"

"Yeah ..." Jared nodded. "Every time."

"Good. Us old 'uns do know a thing or two."

Loud chiming, from the grandfather clock hanging over the window, resounded around the kitchen.

Hyacinth gripped Jared's shoulders, presenting him with an intense gaze. "Time's up. Listen to me, Cupcake. I want you to get up off your butt, kick that demon's ass all the way back to hell and save your friends. No buts, if or any of that talk. Ya hear?"

"Oh, I hear, Grandma, but—"

"Ah, ah. What the heck did I just say?"

"No buts," Jared repeated.

"Exactly. You can do it. Oh, and sorry for this." She slapped him on the right cheek.

"Dang!" Jared rubbed where she hit him.

"Wake up, Jared. *Wake up.*" Hyacinth's voice echoed around him.

Jared gasped, opening his eyes. He felt the back of his head and found a tiny drop of blood on his fingers.

Hyacinth's pep talk repeated in his mind. He groaned while getting to his feet.

How am I gonna find them now? They're way ahead. Then he remembered another part of his gift he inherited from Hyacinth: psychometry.

Jared glanced around at all the trees. One stood out, almost calling to him.

"Guess this must be the one."

He walked slowly, as his back was racked with pain. Clearing his mind of any thoughts, Jared meditated as he touched the tree. His fingers felt the rough grooves of the bark. Nothing came to him, no images of Jessica or her father running to a safe spot.

Dammit, come on! Focus.

Jared tried again, listening to his breathing. After a few seconds, he saw the Barlows fleeing and Malik weaving in and out between trees, gaining on them. Next he saw a lake—one that his dad used to take him to on fishing trips when he was younger.

Jared knew exactly where they were.

"Hold on, guys, I'm coming. God help me."

Jared winced and groaned, only able to run at half his usual speed. Every step sent a jolt up his spine.

***

A strong, dense sensation fell around Jessica and her father as they continued running. She had called out to him to stop, but he'd kept going. Now he came to a halt, bent over, hands on knees.

"Dad, why did you run?" Jess scolded. "We were safe."

"Safe? Stones started levitating and shot at us," Bill replied in disbelief.

"Did we get hit by any? No, because we were protected inside the circle."

"You might be used to this, but I'm not. How can you stay so calm?"

"I trust Jared, and he knows what he's doing. We need to go

back to him. Like, right now."

Someone whistling a familiar nursery rhyme made both of them go rigid. The whistling was loud, piercing, and its echoes bounced off the trees. The tune swirled around them like a tornado. The wind increased, blowing leaves, and any litter that happened to be strewn around, their way.

"Get behind me, Jess," Bill warned, shielding her with his body.

Manic laughter replaced the whistling, growing louder and louder. Jessica glanced around, seeking out its source, but deep down she knew who it was.

They retreated further, their heads turning left and right, searching for any viable exit.

Suddenly, the laughter ended. A tall, handsome man in an expensive-looking suit emerged from behind a tree.

"Dad, be careful," Jessica whispered.

"Do you know him?" Bill asked.

"No, but I think he might be a demon."

"Well, hello there," the man said. "Nice day for a stroll." He took out a cigar from inside his suit jacket. "Do you mind?" he asked, raising the cigar.

"What do you want?" Bill said.

"I take that as a no." Malik clipped off the end of the cigar. When it was in his mouth, he winked, and it was lit. Smoke rose from it. "It's a dirty habit, I know."

"Leave me and my daughter alone," Bill shouted.

"Oh, *now* you want to be the protective father? Where were you the last eight years, when dear, sweet Jessica there needed one?"

Jessica stepped out from behind Bill and confronted Malik. "Look, my dad already said he'd turn himself in, and he will. Just let us go. All this can end right now."

"Yes, yes, I know. And you're right, it can end now." A ravenous smile spread unnaturally wide across Malik's face. "And it will."

He made a swatting motion with the left hand, catapulting Jessica into the nearby tree trunk and pinning her up against it. Her arms and legs spread out. Tight, invisible restraints prevented her from moving.

"Let me go," she demanded.

"Son of a—" Bill roared, charging at the demon.

"Dad, no!" Jessica bellowed but he didn't listen.

Bill swung left and right, hitting nothing but air, the entity deftly dodging every blow with supernatural speed.

"Oooh, such anger," Malik taunted. Bill bought the bait, swinging even harder, again missing his target.

"Enough games." Malik caught Bill's fist with his right hand and squeezed. The crunching of bones accompanied Bill's screaming.

"Stop it!" Jessica pleaded through watery eyes.

The demon bent down, his face an inch away from Bill's. "I won't stop until you're dead." With his left hand, he picked the man up. Bill tried to break free by kicking and wriggling.

"Fly, little birdie. Fly!"

Malik hurled Bill through the air. He hit a few trees before falling to the ground.

"Woohoo! That was fun. Let's go again."

Malik raised both hands like an orchestra conductor, waving them about. Bill was hauled up once more, floating in mid-air.

From where she was, Jessica could see that he was barely conscious. There was a deep gash above his right eye, and his head bobbed as he tried to stay conscious.

Bill was cast about again, bouncing off another four trees. As he struck the last one, there was a loud crack, like a stick or a piece of wood being snapped in half.

Jessica's father lay in a heap, crying in agony, holding his left leg.

"Don't touch him again. Hasn't he suffered enough already?" Jessica said.

"Not enough for my liking."

The demon glided, off the ground, to where Bill lay. Bill covered his head as the evil entity landed beside him.

"Aw, look at the poor little puppy," Malik said in pseudo-sympathy. "Do you know what the best thing to do is when a dog's no longer useful?" He leaned in closer, his face morphing into its true, hideous form, a being with pitch-black, leathery skin and luminous orange veins. "You put it down."

"Back off!" Jared shouted, shakily throwing some holy water at Malik. The demon recoiled as some of it sizzled on his suit.

Jared thrust the crucifix in front of him. "Sa—Saint Michael the Archangel, de—defend us in battle—"

"You won't win this time!" Malik blew a breath which transformed into a strong gale, knocking Jared off his feet.

Doubt flooded the boy's mind again. *He's too strong. I won't be able to beat him.*

Then, Hyacinth's advice drowned out the negative thoughts. *You're stronger than him because God's on your side. Let your faith shine through. Kick Mr. Nasty's ass.*

Malik placed a foot on Jared's chest. It felt like a boulder had been dropped on him and his breastbone would cave in, at any second, under its weight.

"Normally, I'd give the courtesy of letting someone say their last words. But in your case, I'll pass."

Malik's eyes glowed a fiery red. He lifted his leg, ready to drive it through Jared's heart.

"Oh, God," Jared cried.

"He's not going to save you now."

Jared felt a tingling sensation up his spine.

They weren't alone.

Malik clearly noticed it, too, and looked behind him.

"Oh, so you've decided to join the party?" Malik said.

Tabitha stood there, hands by her sides like a cowboy ready to draw his guns. "Let them go. This has gone on long enough. No more."

"And spoil the fun? No thanks."

"I wasn't asking."

Tabitha launched herself at Malik. The two tumbled and tussled on the ground, becoming nothing more than a white-and-navy blur.

"Jared, over here," Jessica cried out.

Jared got up and ran over to where she was. He recited the Archangel Michael Protection Prayer while sprinkling some water where her limbs were bound; and, after saying the prayer three times, Jessica was freed.

"Oh, thank God," she said, massaging her wrists. "We need to get my dad out of here."

Just as they were about to sprint to him, Tabitha and Malik stopped their brawling right in front of them. Malik caught the woman by the throat, holding her several feet off the ground.

"You're really beginning to bore me." Malik head-butted her twice. Each time he connected, it was like a crash of thunder.

Malik let Tabitha go. She fell to the ground, no longer offering any resistance.

"Now, where were we?" Malik slowly turned around to face Jared and Jessica. A red glow flared in his eyes again. "Ah, yes."

Jared held the crucifix like a sword. Sunlight glinted off its golden frame. "I command you in, Jesus' name, to—"

"Oh, shut up." Malik waved a hand, knocking the crucifix out of Jared's grip.

As Malik came closer to him, Jared threw some holy water on Malik's face.

The demon reeled back, covering it with his hands. Jared seized the opportunity and grabbed the cross. He marched forward, determination taking the place of fear in his body.

Malik wiped the water off. "I'll end this now, and not even your God will save you."

Jared walked on, defiant, rattling off the Archangel Michael Prayer. He doused more water on Malik. A quick check of the bottle revealed that he didn't have much left.

Malik blew another gale at him, but Jared rooted his feet to the ground and was only pushed back a few inches. He threw another splash of liquid at Malik, this time making the demon retreat.

In Jared's peripheral vision, he saw Tabitha stir and look at him.

"I know you can hear me," she said telepathically. "How can I help?"

"I need salt. It's in my backpack," Jared replied, never averting his gaze from Malik.

Tabitha disappeared, and Jared kept sprinkling Malik with the remainder of the holy water. The forest rang with Malik's agonized cries, each drop hitting him as if it were a whip. Lash marks spread across his skin, and orange goo oozed from the wounds.

Malik let loose a guttural growl and swung both arms. Jared ducked, feeling a strong breeze graze his hair.

An icy chill on his neck let him know Tabitha had returned.

"Salt is behind you," she said in his mind.

"Thanks."

Jared picked it up. Glancing at Jessica, he threw the salt at her, and she caught it.

"Make a circle around him!" Jared yelled.

Jessica gave him an incredulous "are you serious?" look.

"Now, Jess!" Jared insisted.

Jessica jumped into action, giving the demon a wide berth and pouring salt, making a large circle. When she was finished, she ran behind Jared.

"That should hold him," Jared said.

Soon, the wind died down. Malik looked pitiful, with his suit torn and cuts covering his battered body.

Jared stood an inch outside the circle, staring him in the eyes. The crucifix now shone brighter as he continued saying the prayer.

"No!" Malik roared, twisting his head in every direction, trying to fight Jared's onslaught. "Damn you ... Damn ... your ... God ..." Flakes of skin peeled off Malik's face, leaving only a dark shadow behind.

The ground underneath Jared's feet trembled. Part of him became afraid, and he swallowed nervously; but a calmness washed over him, urging the boy to continue.

Jared cast the last drop on Malik.

The demon unleashed a shout, similar to a herd of elephants crying in unison, as his body shook so vigorously he was nothing more than a mere blur.

Jared and Jessica hit the ground, covering their ears.

"NOOOO!" Malik yelled.

His body exploded.

A deafening stillness fell over the forest, the leaves no longer whirling about in the wind. The branches ceased swaying.

Jessica, scanning her surroundings, risked raising her head.

"Is it ... over?"

Jared removed the hand covering his head. It was his turn to see if the coast was clear.

"Yeah ... guess so."

There, inside the salty circle, was a mound of ashes. Jared's instincts told him to say one more prayer. When he was finished, they blazed and disappeared, leaving only a wisp of smoke in their place.

"Let's get your dad," he said.

Jared helped Jessica up, and they ran to where Bill lay. There was a circular red patch on the right leg of his pants.

"Damn leg's broken. Can't walk on it. Wrist's hurt too," he informed them, confirming what Jared thought.

"All right, but we can't leave him here. We've gotta try and bring him back to town," Jared said.

"Let me see if I can call an ambulance." Jessica took out her phone. She frowned. "Crap. There's no signal out here."

"Makes sense. Me and my dad could never get any when we went fishing. Come on, help me lift him up," Jared said.

It took a few minutes to get Bill to his feet. Jared, working one-handed, proved a hindrance also. Once his arms were around Jared and Jessica's shoulders, they walked to the car.

Although confident that Malik was defeated, Jared still swept his surroundings with a watchful gaze.

When they reached the car, Jessica gingerly placed Bill in the front seat and drove to the hospital.

Jared sat in the back seat, breathing a sigh of relief, glad that another case was almost closed and his friend's family was safe.

PART FIVE: CLOSURE

Jessica sat in the hospital cafeteria finishing her dinner. Now she knew why everyone hated the food here. It tasted bland, like it was just microwaved five minutes before serving.

Over the last few weeks, between visiting Jared, Bertha and now Bill, the hospital had become her second home. The doctors told her that her dad had sustained serious fractures, and they would take months to heal. Bill would be wheelchair-bound for the foreseeable future.

When he had heard this, an amalgamation of emotions had been evident on his face, from disappointment and anguish to fury.

After the Caleb Hammerson haunting, Jessica had thought nothing would ever be worse than that.

Boy, was I wrong.

Jared wandered in with Bertha behind him.

Jessica's mother faked a smile as she sat opposite her. Jessica knew her mom was putting on a brave face, hiding the pain and strain evident in the dark circles around her eyes, the tiredness showing in her sluggish movements.

Jared stayed standing.

"Do you guys want a soda or coffee?" he asked.

"No, I'm good," Bertha replied.

Jessica pointed to the half-full plastic cup beside her plate. "Thanks, but I already have one."

"Cool. Be back in a sec."

Jared went to the coffee machine.

"He told me about your dad," Bertha said to her daughter. "You were extremely lucky, Jess."

"I know. It was touch and go, but we did it. Just hope Dad will be okay."

"Does he still want to ... you know ...?"

"Turn himself in? Yeah. Said it again this morning."

"And how do you feel about it?"

"Not good. I'm even more worried about what happens if he doesn't."

"Yeah ... seems like you all had a real rumble in the forest." Bertha paused. "Jared said it was like fightin' Mike Tyson, Floyd

Mayweather and a whole slew of others out there."

"Bad doesn't even start to cover it, Mom. I thought ..." Jessica's voice broke, her lips trembling.

Bertha reached over to hold her hand. "Let it out, girl."

Jessica put down the fork. "I thought we were gonna die. I've never seen so much evil." She furtively wiped away a tear and cleared her throat.

"Thank God you got through that."

"Thing is, Dad will have to turn himself in. If he doesn't, we're screwed. But just as I was getting to know him, he gets taken away."

"I know, and it's crappy that he has to do this." Bertha looked away, trying to conceal her own tears. "This is all my fault. If I hadn't drank too much that night and fooled around .... we all ..."

Her words couldn't come out as she was choked up with emotion. She had to fix her gaze to the floor while trying to maintain some composure.

Jessica pushed away the plate and what remained on it, no longer having any interest in eating.

"So ... what now?" she asked.

"Just be there as much as we can for your dad during his recovery," Bertha said. "Did he say when he'd contact the police?"

"In a few days' time, he's phoning Detective Ramirez."

Bertha squeezed Jessica's hand again. "I don't like it either, honey, but you need me."

"Easy for you to say. You're not the one going to prison."

Bertha hunched over, choking down a sob.

Jessica instantly regretted her words. "Sorry, Mom. I'm just tired, scared, hurt ..."

"Aren't we all, honey? Look, let's go home. Tomorrow, we can come back and see your dad again."

Jessica nodded in agreement. There wasn't much energy in her for a fight.

This whole situation felt weird to her. Last night, she'd cried for hours, wishing it was another family going through this dilemma. She hoped that the judge might show some leniency on her father; but after hearing so many bad stories about the justice system, she didn't hold out much hope.

***

The parking lot was quiet as Bertha sat in her car. On the front passenger seat was a bottle of Irish whiskey in a brown paper bag. The pressure had been building up over the last week, and old cravings had returned. All along, she'd felt the need for a drink gnawing away at the back of her mind, tempting her into breaking her vow to never touch alcohol again. As Tabitha's and the demon's attacks grew worse, the bottles of liquor called to her more and more, almost beckoning Bertha to take just one little sip.

What harm would it do, right? Just one small drop. It's not like you'd be drinking the whole bottle or anything. These were the thoughts that plagued her on a daily basis. Despite all that, it was her bond with Jessica and the love she had for her that stopped Bertha from giving in.

All that had changed today, seeing Bill in the hospital and knowing the next step he was going to take. Guilt racked her like it never had before.

With the paper bag half pulled down, the golden, caramel-colored liquid glimmered in the sunlight. Bertha could feel her pulse race and her lips go dry. Grabbing the bottle, she unscrewed it, letting the whiskey's smell invade her nostrils. She sucked the aroma in. Bringing the bottle to her mouth, the intoxicating liquid flowed ever closer to her lips, now only mere inches away.

As the whiskey was about to swim down her throat, images of happy times with Jessica played like a slideshow in Bertha's mind. Memories of days spent at a spa or the movies, or even at home, sitting beside each other and sharing a bowl of popcorn while watching a DVD, caused a stirring inside her. These were moments they should have shared ever since Bill left; but for years, she'd let Jessica live in fear.

What am I doing? Do I really want to throw all that away now we're close again?

Bertha spat out whatever alcohol had entered her mouth, immediately opening the door. Turning the bottle upside down, she poured all the whiskey onto the damp ground.

This really is all my fault. I gotta make this whole thing right, and there's only one way to do that.

Her course of action was clear now. Bertha just hoped that she'd have enough courage inside to do it.

***

Jessica finished filling the second cup of coffee for Bill from the machine. As she stirred it, the vision she received of him being attacked in the men's room haunted her. There were numerous times she'd wanted to talk to Jared about it and get his advice. Then doubts would pop up, and Jessica would wonder if it was all her imagination, despite what she saw in her mind having actually happened.

Did she have some hidden power? None of her family ever had abilities like that, so why her?

I really have to speak to Jared about this, Jessica thought, throwing the plastic spoon into the trash can. She brought the coffee to her father's room.

Bill's face lit up as Jessica walked in. He put aside the newspaper he was reading.

"Thanks for the coffee."

"No problem. It doesn't taste great, but I've had worse."

"Well, it's the hospital, not Starbucks," Bill said.

"That's for sure."

Bill took a sip and put the cup up on the windowsill, since it was closer than his bedside locker.

He cleared his throat. "Listen, Jess, there's something I wanna say."

Uh-oh, here we go, she thought.

"Coming back here and spending time with you has been great, even better than that. The hauntings and having my leg and wrist broken by a demon, not so much," he joked, to ease the tension.

Jessica chuckled. Inside, though, she was bracing for whatever was about to come.

"I really wish I came back sooner and spent more time with you. I'll regret that for the rest of my life."

"Sorry, Dad … I don't mean to be rude, but can you get to the point?"

"You know we have to make things right."

She nodded.

"So in order for me to do that, I gotta make that call today."

"You mean, the police?"

"Uh-huh." Bill held her hand for support. "And I want you there with me when I do."

"Dad ... I really don't want you to do this, but I know we have to."

"Let me guess, you'd rather we figure out another way, right? Have you or Jared thought of one?" Bill asked.

Jessica shook her head.

"Then I have to do this. It's the only way to make sure you and your mom are safe. It should've been done a long time ago, but we were both scared."

"I understand. I guess the Logans deserve some closure, too."

"It's long overdue, Jess. If anything happened you I'd never forgive myself, and neither would your mom." Bill pointed to his small, compact locker. "Can you give me my phone, please?"

Jessica took it out and handed him the cell.

"Do you have the number?"

"Yeah, it's right here," Bill replied, lifting up the newspaper he had been reading as she arrived.

"Before you do, Dad, can I say something?"

"Sure."

"No matter what happens, I'll be with you all the way."

Bill wiped away a tear that was about to roll off her chin.

"Come here. Give your old man a big one."

Jessica hugged him tight. She didn't want to let her father go and wished they could stay together forever.

"All right, Slugger." Bill patted her twice on the back to break the embrace. "Let's get this over with."

Jessica let him go.

Bill turned the pages in the newspaper, stopping when he found the picture of Detective Ramirez and a number to call him on.

"Here's the moment of truth."

They held hands again as he punched in the number on his cell.

"Bill, stop," Bertha said.

Jessica and her father looked up to see her standing in the doorway.

"Mom, what are you doing here?" Jessica said. "You should be resting."

"I'm here to stop your dad making a mistake. I already ruined your lives once before. I won't sit by and do it again."

"What do you mean?" Bill's eyes narrowed in confusion.

"It was my fault we killed Tabitha that night. I distracted you and we hit her. It was me who kept you away from Jess all these years. So it should be me who should pay the price."

Jessica got up, her face awash with puzzlement. "What are you saying, Mom? You're turning yourself in?"

"Yeah ... I am ... later today," Bertha replied.

"W—Why the sudden change of heart?" Jessica asked.

"Your dad was the most precious thing in the world. I took that away from you eight years ago. He should never have left but he did because of me. Jess, there's something you have to know. Your dad, he sent letters, and I—"

"Hid them?" Jessica finished her mother's sentence. "Yes, I know. Dad told me a few days ago. I was gonna talk about it but … I can't be without you, Mom."

"You won't be alone. Your dad will be here. Where he belongs."

Bill put down the cell and sat up straight. "Bertha, I know you feel guilty about what happened. So do I, but Jess is right: she needs a mother. She got by without me."

"No, she didn't," Bertha replied. "I made her life *hell* for seven years—"

"But—" Jessica interjected, but Bertha held up a hand to signal

127

to let her finish.

"The last twelve months have been the best we've had since 2012, but I couldn't live with myself if I ripped your dad away from you again."

"Bertha, please think about this," Bill pleaded. "You may never get out of jail, or see the outside world again, for twenty-five years."

"We all knew that somebody had to take the fall, and it's gotta be me. Face it, you wouldn't last long in there. I don't wanna go to jail either; but out of the two of us, I'd last longer."

Bill laughed while shrugging his shoulders.

Bertha cupped Jessica's freckled cheeks in her hands. "I'm so sorry for all the pain I've caused. You're a fantastic daughter, and you've done me and your dad proud all these years. But as a parent, I've gotta set an example. Own my mistakes. Today, I'm gonna do just that. It was my idea to bury her in that field and dump the car in the lake. We robbed the Logan family of some happy years with Tabitha. That's all on me."

"I was the one driving, Bertha. All this is partially my fault too," he added.

"True, but I was fooling around. You looked away at a vital moment because of me. At the end of the day, it all comes back to me ... so I should be the one to pay. This should've been done back then, not now."

"Mom ... I really don't want—" Jessica caught herself, trying not to cry.

"I know, honey, but I have to." Bertha squeezed Jessica in her arms. "Your dad deserves you more than I do. He's suffered enough as it is."

Jessica pulled back, wiping her mother's tears away. "I know we've had our ups and downs, but you're a great mom. I'll always love you. I promise I'll come visit every week."

"Thank you, baby." Bertha kissed her forehead. "There's one thing I wanna ask you first."

"Sure," Jessica replied, dabbing at her own tears, now.

"Will you come to the station? I feel like I need someone with me."

"Of course I will," Jessica said and gave her mother another hug.

"Bertha, are you sure about this?"

Bertha went over to Bill and held his hand. "Nothing's been clearer in my life. Besides, you need to be there for her. No girl should be without her daddy."

"Don't worry, I'll take real good care of her. Have you thought about what you're gonna say?"

"Yeah, got it thought out."

"Maybe we should nail down this story first, before you go?" Bill suggested. "Just so there's no holes in it."

"Guess you're right." Bertha turned to Jessica. "I think we're gonna need another cup of coffee."

"Don't worry. I'll get it."

Jessica walked out of the room. Just as she was about to go down to the coffee machine, she stopped, looking back in. Bertha hugged Bill while saying a tearful, "I'm sorry." Bill rubbed her back before becoming misty-eyed himself.

Jessica knew that there was a long road ahead for both her parents, but she was going to make damn sure that she'd be there for them.

***

Although he'd been living in Hopps Town all his life, the view from Bunker Hill never failed to amaze Jared. The scene in front of him was like something in a painting: a plethora of houses, the stores and cafés on Main Street, and the magnificent building that was Hopps Town High. Beyond that was the main attraction of beautiful mountains and forests, all illuminated by glorious sunshine.

An hour ago, Jessica had told him about her mother turning herself in. Jared knew if this case was to be closed, there was one more act to be carried out. For this he'd need advice. He just hoped Maybelle would be able to answer his call.

Tapping the Facetime icon on the phone, he hit Maybelle's name. Jared waited for his aunt to answer.

Finally, her face, filled with tiredness, appeared.

"Hey, nephew. What's up?"

"I'm good, thanks," Jared said. "You?"

"So-so. Still in hospital."

"Yeah, I get that. Thanks for the warning, by the way."

"That's what I'm here for. Did you get him?"

"Sure did. Was tough, though. That dude went down swinging."

"Most of them always do. Hey, take a look at this."

Maybelle turned her phone around to show some decorative artwork of flowers and bright red ladybugs on her cast.

Jared laughed. "I see you were busy."

"Oh, please. I'm going insane in here. If I have to do another word puzzle I'll scream."

"I won't be giving my dad one of those for you, so ..."

"No, please don't. How come I get the feeling this ain't a social call, J?" Maybelle asked in a concerned tone.

"Nothing gets past you, huh?"

Maybelle shook her head with a broad smile.

"Now the demon's gone, I want to help Tabitha cross over. She deserves that, after all this crap."

"Okay. Let me guess, you don't know what to say to the family, though?" Maybelle asked.

"Bingo."

"Just say who you are and what you do. No need to be embarrassed or ashamed of your gift," Maybelle said.

Try telling them that. He imagined what their response would be—probably one of skepticism and anger.

"Yeah, but what if she blows me off as another crazy psychic?" he said.

"Then if that's what happens, so be it. But you'll never know unless you try. It's always possible to do it without them; but for real closure and peace of mind, get the parents involved."

"Yeah. Guess you're right."

"You say that like it only just occurred to you," Maybelle retorted playfully.

Jared chuckled.

"Yo, thanks, Aunt Belle. I appreciate it, as always."

"I'll be looking forward to that dinner you owe me next time we meet."

"Looking forward to it too. Rest up. Love ya."

"Bring it home, J. I know you can do it. Ciao." Maybelle blew a kiss back at him and hung up.

Jared sat back in his seat. Butterflies fluttered in his stomach; and, for a moment, he thought he would vomit. Taking out a piece of paper with Imelda Logan's number on it, which he'd found in an old phonebook earlier that day, he sucked in a deep breath.

After typing in the digits, his finger hovered over the green icon. With another breath to brace himself, Jared tapped it.

An elderly lady answered after four rings.

"Um ... hi. Is this Imelda Logan?"

"Yes ..." she answered warily.

"My name is J—Jared Duval. I'm calling about your daughter Tabitha ..."

***

Jared sat in the car, saying prayers and listening to his favorite music, trying to build up the courage to go up and ring Imelda Logan's doorbell. At first, when he called her, she was skeptical, thinking it was an unscrupulous psychic preying on a vulnerable woman. But when Jared explained that his only intention was to help Tabitha cross over, Imelda slowly believed him. They'd arranged for the ritual to take place at 4 p.m. the next day, when Anna would be at a friend's house. Imelda explained that she'd prefer Anna not to be there, as she thought Anna was too young to understand what had to be done.

"I guess it's the moment of truth," Jared muttered to himself while getting out of the car. He brought a small plastic bottle of holy water with him.

Jared took a deep lungful of air before pressing the white button. A chime rang out and a door was opened further down the hallway.

The figure of a woman approached. She had long, bedraggled dirty-blonde hair with traces of gray running through it. Her leopard-skin glasses were a fraction too big for her attractive face. A white-and-red-checkered shirt fell down over her denim jeans.

"Hi. Imelda?"

"Yes. Are you Jared?"

"Yes ma'am. I am."

"You're not what I was expecting. Someone a little older, maybe." Imelda stepped back, opening the door fully. "Please, come in."

Jared nodded in appreciation and entered. He stared at the eye-catching photos adorning the hallway walls. In them were moments of nature's true beauty, with close-up shots of flowers caught in a slight breeze and fields of wheat stalks painted with a golden illumination from the sun.

"Did you take those?" he asked, pointing to the pictures.

"Yes," Imelda shut the door. "Photography is something I always loved, but only took it seriously recently."

"You got a good eye."

"Thanks. Is it okay if we get on with whatever it is you gotta do to help Tabitha?"

Jared understood her apprehension. He felt it too.

"Uh, sure, Mrs. Logan. Where would you like to do it?"

Imelda thought for a moment and then replied, "How about the backyard? Tabitha loved the outdoors."

"If that's what you want." He caught her examining the small bottle in his hand. "This is holy water. I bring it for extra protection. Do you have a candle we could use?"

"Think so. I'll go get it. The backyard's out that way."

Jared walked through the kitchen, exiting the back door.

The first thing to greet him was a blue trampoline in the center of her backyard.

Jared unscrewed the top from the bottle. He doused the yard, making the sign of the cross in the four corners. He mumbled a few prayers Maybelle taught him while sprinkling.

Imelda returned with a single white beeswax candle. "Will this do?"

"Yeah, that's cool." Jared sprinkled one more spot, lowering his head in prayer. When he was finished, Imelda lit the candle with a cigarette lighter, shielding the flame with her hand.

"So, what now?" she asked.

"I just need to call on Tabitha."

"And just so we're clear, this isn't gonna cost me anything?" Imelda asked.

"No ma'am. I'm not that kind of person." He didn't mention that he was doing this, in a way, to make up for the Barlows' actions eight years ago, even though he knew nothing would ever truly atone for what they did.

"Tabitha ... Tabitha Logan, where are you, girl? Can you please come here?" Jared made a quick inspection of his surroundings, unable to sense anything. "Tabitha ... can you—"

"All right, I'm here," Tabitha said, making Jared leap with fright.

"Damn, you scared me there," he replied, smoothing down his hair.

"What's going on?" Imelda asked, her brow furrowed in concern.

"It's okay, Mrs. Logan. Tabitha's here. She just startled me, that's all."

"Is she really?" There was a hint of excitement in her voice.

Jared nodded the affirmative.

"What does she look like?" Imelda's words were filled with eagerness.

He described her clothes. The girl radiated peace. Today she wore a sparkling white dress, and there was a small bronze brooch in the shape of a spider on her right shoulder.

"I gave her that when she turned eighteen," Imelda said, in a mixture of shock and happiness. "Does she still have black hair?"

"Yes, Mrs. Logan."

"Can I say something to her?" Tabitha asked.

"Sure." Jared explained that her daughter wanted to say something when she gave him a puzzled look

"Tell Mom that she's done a great job raising Anna."

Jared relayed the message.

"Also, can you tell her not to worry about me? I know she's afraid that I'm alone, but I'm okay."

"Tabitha says not to worry about her. She's doing fine."

Imelda stared in the direction Jared looked at when talking to Tabitha. "Is she there?" Imelda said, indicating with her right index finger to his left side.

"Yup."

Imelda walked to the spot while still protecting the flame. She reached out; a broad grin of awe spread across her face. "I can feel ... something."

Tabitha stroked her mother's left cheek.

Imelda gasped. "Is that her?"

"Sure is."

"Wow." She wiped a tear before taking a few steps back again.

Tabitha wiped some of her own.

"Tell Mom I miss her every day, and I'll always be around for her and Anna."

Jared passed it on.

"I miss you too, baby. I still play 'Living On a Prayer' on your birthday." Imelda then turned to Jared. "That was a little tradition we had. We are ... were big Bon Jovi fans. Every year, since she turned eleven, we'd play that song and dance together."

Jared imagined mother and daughter dancing in the kitchen or living room, singing out of tune but, above all, being happy.

"I remember that," Tabitha replied. "Mom always hit the high notes; I never could. I know she worries about Anna, too. Tell her not to. Anna's gonna do well. She's better at school than I was."

"Tabitha says Anna's gonna be just fine at school. So stop worrying."

"It was always my biggest regret Tabitha never got a proper education," Imelda confessed. "I hated myself every day for her not getting a diploma."

"It wasn't Mom's fault. She tried to warn me, but I didn't listen, as usual," Tabitha conceded.

"She never blamed you and wishes she listened to you more."

"I heard on the radio that woman who knocked you down turned herself in. So now you can finally rest in peace, sweetie," Imelda said.

Jared noticed from the mother's expression that she struggled to remain composed.

A swooshing sound made Jared look behind him. There, a few inches away from Tabitha, was a door of rippling white light.

"Is that my ride home?" Tabitha asked.

"Sure is," Jared answered.

"Thank you for this." She touched his hand in appreciation. "I know this doesn't mean much to you now, but I'm sorry about Bill getting hurt. I wanted to make those people suffer, but I didn't want to kill them. That was all Malik's idea."

"I understand and I'm sorry about what happened to you, Tabitha. It's safe to go now, though," Jared assured her.

"Bye Mom."

"Tabitha says goodbye."

Imelda's voice broke as she spoke. "Bye, baby."

Tabitha gulped. She wiped away another tear before stepping into the white light. When she was halfway in, she turned around to wave goodbye.

Jared told Imelda what she was doing, and they both waved back.

Tabitha stared at the heavenly horizons before walking fully into the portal. It reduced in size to a mere blip, flickered for a few seconds, and was gone.

When Imelda sensed her daughter had left, she broke down. Jared lent her his shoulder as she leaned into it. He put an arm around the grieving mother.

***

A few evenings later, Jessica sat on the bed in her room, staring out the window. Rain pounded the windowpane, and dull gray clouds blanketed the sky. She felt as miserable as the weather outside. Her thoughts centered on Bertha again, and how she was going to be put away for a very long time.

After they went to the station, Bertha confessed to knocking down and killing Tabitha and burying her body in the field where she was discovered. She said that an old friend who had since passed helped dump the car in Branson Lake—Bill had nothing to do with Tabitha's death.

Bertha was kept in custody after her admission, and would remain there until a date for her sentencing was set. Bill knew that there would be a high bail cost, so Jessica and her dad had to come up with a way to find the money for it, if it was granted. Jessica also had to find a job to help pay the bills at home and buy food. Bill sold his car and tools, as well as giving up most of his life savings to get Bertha out.

Jessica had cried the previous two evenings, but not today. As hard as it would be without her mom around, it would be even harder if she'd been killed by Malik. At least this way, she'd get to see her mom, even if it was only one day a week.

Her cell phone's ringtone snapped her out of deep thought. It was Jared.

"Hey. How did the crossing over go?" Jessica asked.

"It went well. I was so nervous. Never done it with a family member there before."

"I bet it must've been nerve-racking. You did it, though. She's finally at peace," Jessica said.

"Yeah, she is. How's your dad?"

"He's okay but my mom ... not so much. I wish it could've turned out different."

"I know, but it could've been so much worse, too. That Malik was a bad dude, the worst we've faced so far."

"Got that right. Is he gone for good?" Jessica asked.

"Hope so."

Jessica guessed that Jared realized his answer mightn't put her at ease, as he quickly added: "Don't think he'll be coming back anytime soon."

"That's great." Jessica took the opportunity to talk about the vision she'd had at Jackie's. "I know this probably isn't the right time to ask, but there's something I wanna talk about. A week ago, when me and Dad were eating out, he was attacked by Malik."

"Whoa, hold up. How come I'm only hearing about this now?" Jared asked, concern in his voice.

"Can I just finish?" Jessica replied.

"Um, sure. Sorry."

"Thing is, while he was being attacked in the men's room, I was at the table and I kind of had a ... vision."

There was a pause on the other end.

"A *vision?*" Jared asked.

"I don't know how else to describe it. I saw my dad being choked with his scarf. If I hadn't foreseen it, he'd be dead."

"Have you been holding out on me, girl?" Jared asked, halfjokingly.

"It's never happened before. I swear. That's why I'm kind of freaking out."

"Clearly you have some powers, too. And this is the first time?"

"Yup. That was the only time. Do you think maybe it was a one-off?" Jessica hoped to hear that it was.

"I'm not sure. Maybelle told me that sometimes under stress, our abilities show up. Maybe it's time for your powers to kick in. Who knows? Have you told anyone else?"

"No, just you."

"Well, if you need help developing them, maybe we could try together sometime," Jared suggested.

This was a tempting offer—anything to take her mind off the coming trial—but right now wasn't the time. Jessica knew from the two exorcisms Jared had performed that focus was a key component in making these abilities work, and that was something she was finding hard to do.

"Thanks, Jared. I've got so much on my plate right now that I don't think I could do it, but maybe another time?"

"Sure, whatever works for you."

Jessica checked her watch. It was after 4 p.m. and she had to make some dinner.

"I gotta go. Thanks for the call, and I'm so glad the crossing over went well."

"Me too. Catch ya later."

At least one good thing came out of all this, she thought. Now Tabitha could rest in peace. She just wished it hadn't come at the cost of losing her own mother for twenty years, or possibly more.

***

Four Months Later

Cemeteries always gave Jessica an unusual sense of peace. Once, she'd joked with Jared and Adrian that she must have been an undertaker in a previous life because she felt so at ease in them.

She sat on the freshly painted cream bench at Hopps Town's New Cemetery. In her hand, Jessica held a single red rose meant for Tabitha's grave. She had wanted to pay a visit for a while, but kept delaying it—after all, there had been plenty to keep her busy.

College had taken a back seat during the hauntings, despite her managing to squeeze in a few hours' study every day. When Bill came home to recover, a lot of Jessica's time was taken up helping her father get around the house or cooking his meals. Jessica arrived at the realization that she wasn't going back to school, at least not right now, and she'd asked for a one-year deferral. The admissions board granted her request, but she sensed from the wording of their email that it was with a great deal of reluctance.

And then, of course, there was her mom's trial and sentencing. That caused a sensation in Hopps Town. For a week leading up to the court case, media vans had camped outside the Barlows' home, and the family soon felt as if they were under house arrest. Bertha had put on a brave face, always joking.

Bill put all his energy into getting better, attending every physiotherapy session he was offered. His hard work paid off: he was walking again, without the aid of a crutch, in just four months, quicker than doctors had expected. His wrist healed well, too.

A week before the court date, and when she was alone in Jessica's company, Bertha caved, revealing her true feelings. Some days she broke down, telling all her fears about being in jail and all the horrible things that could happen to her in there. But Bertha maintained that she would fare better in prison than her ex-husband, even though prison was the last place she wanted to be.

The fateful day arrived. Jessica remembered cameras almost blinding her with their flashes; Bertha being led into the court house by an army of police officers while other cops held eager reporters at bay; and the sour-faced, double-jawed judge taking his seat as they entered the court room.

The silence in the room was deafening, save for the odd cough. Judge Cornwell's beady eyes scanned the paper in front of him before switching to Bertha. His final statement often replayed in Jessica's mind, and she knew it would haunt her forever.

"Mrs. Barlow, I know it took great courage to finally turn yourself in, and for that I commend you. However, what you did eight years ago, whether by accident or willful intent, robbed a family of a daughter and mother. But to conceal that crime—and to make Mrs. Logan and her granddaughter suffer, not knowing, for all this time, what happened to the woman they loved and cherished—was almost as despicable as the act itself. I hereby sentence you to twenty-five years' imprisonment in Hopps Town Penitentiary, to be served with immediate effect." He then cast a softer gaze to Imelda. "I hope now, Mrs. Logan, that you and your family can finally find some peace, knowing justice was served today. Take the prisoner away."

Jessica would never be able to erase from her mind the shame on Bertha's face as she was led out by the officers. Jessica promised to keep in touch; and, in just a few days, she was visiting her mother in jail for the first time.

Bill was quiet for the first week or so after the trial. Jessica could see that he felt bad for his ex-wife: she noticed that his face always had a sullen expression when he thought she couldn't see him. He tried to keep up a brave face by preparing dinner and renting movies they'd loved to watch when she was a kid, but there was always sadness and regret dwelling in his eyes.

Jared texted Jessica every day to check in on her, even when he went back to college. She was grateful to him, because she could only really open up to Jared—she didn't want to add to the heavy weight of guilt Bill carried on his shoulders.

Can't stay here forever, Jessica thought as she got up. She walked past many headstones until coming to Tabitha's grave. A colorful floral wreath, reading *Mom*, lay across it. Other flowers and bouquets were also scattered around. Jessica bent down, adding her rose.

"This is gonna sound like a broken record but I'm sorry about what my parents did, Tabitha," she said. "I hope you're finally resting in peace."

A huge sense of relief washed over Jessica, a calmness infiltrating every pore of her body.

Does this mean she forgives us?

A little robin landed on top of the headstone, chirping a short song before flying away again. To Jessica, this was a sign that Tabitha had finally pardoned them, and that she had, at last, found eternal peace.

US Military Base—Location Unknown

The glare of General Tom Beckford's computer screen illuminated his face as he finished a report. His wrists were sore and stiff from typing for the last hour without a break.

Old habits die hard, Tom thought, remembering those sessions he had in his younger days when working for the high school paper, typing up stories for hours on end. It would take so long to do because he used only two fingers on an old typewriter.

The office Tom found himself in now was much grander than the tight, compact space at home. The desk was nearly seven feet wide, with plenty of room for the globe sitting on the left. Stationery, files and folders were littered around the computer—tidiness was something the general often strived for but seldom achieved, what with the amount of folders and envelopes that came his way every day.

Two American flags stood behind him on either side of his chair. There was not much space on the walls for family pictures, save for a few of his father, a former admiral, and some grandkids. Two other great generals from the past, Patton and MacArthur—men he particularly admired—took up prominent positions on the left and right walls. On his desk, there was a photo of three generations of soldiers from the Beckford family: Grandpa Beckford, a retired lieutenant and Korean War veteran, his father, Al, and a younger Tom, who'd been a newly promoted private first class when the snap was taken. All three men were in their respective uniforms.

Tilting his white mug, which also featured a picture of the US flag, revealed that more tea was needed. Just as Tom was about to get up, the cell phone rang.

"Hello?"

"The weapon is ready. The trial will begin in ten minutes," a soft-spoken female informed him.

"Thanks, Dr. Hodges. I'll be right down."

Tom stood up, put on his blue uniform jacket, which he'd hung on the back of the chair, and slipped his cap on over his ash-blond hair.

That tea will have to wait.

This trial was something he had been looking forward to all day. Soldiers in the hallway, dressed in army fatigues, stood to attention, saluting him as he walked passed. The shadow from Tom's tall, broad frame loomed large as he walked through the dull gray unpainted corridors to the only elevator on the floor.

Tom pressed the "call elevator" button, surrounding it in a green halo. The silver doors opened and Tom stepped in.

There was no need to press anything inside, since it was programmed to take only high-ranking officials, like himself, to Floor 20. Some scientists in the Research and Development Department called that place the "Lower Floor of Hell", but Tom had nicknamed it his "Playhouse".

Tom looked at his reflection in the elevator's silver interior. Helen, his mother, often remarked that he looked a lot like his father, with the same long face and intensive gaze. As time had gone on, and from what Tom now saw in front of him, he had to agree.

"You have arrived at Floor 20," a computer-generated female voice announced. The doors opened, and Dr. Miranda Hodges—a fair-skinned woman of medium height, with brown eyes, black hair tied up in a ponytail, and wearing a white doctor's coat and French beige skirt—greeted him. She held a clipboard and three thick, padded manila envelopes to her chest.

"Dr. Hodges. Good to see you again," Tom said as they made their way to the Observation Room.

"Thank you, General, sir," Hodges replied. "The Exercise Room is prepped. Here are the three test subjects."

Miranda handed him the heavy envelopes, and Tom opened the first one. It contained a folder, inside which was the profile of "Subject One", Ted Morrison. A picture of a vicious-looking, red-haired man in his mid-thirties was stapled to the top left-hand corner of the front page. From reading the file, Tom learned that Ted was a former Navy Seal who'd been dishonorably discharged.

"Let's see what's behind Door Number Two ..." Tom muttered.

The second file was that of Matt Smyth, a short, bald twenty-nine-year-old Special Forces sniper who was jailed for brawling with—and killing—a fellow soldier while on leave. File three described Hannah Montrose, a forty-something, well-toned African American woman. A former police officer, she'd been terminated and imprisoned for extreme brutality against a handcuffed perpetrator.

"So Subjects Two and Three are prisoners?" Tom asked.

"Yes, sir."

"And they've been released as part of the terms of the 'Exercise Agreement'?"

"Yes. They've been carefully vetted by our team."

"So how did our recruiter spin it to them?"

"Subjects Two and Three were promised early release as part of a special mission to test weapons for the armed forces. All three are incredibly patriotic."

"That's the way I like it."

Miranda and Tom arrived at the Observation Room. The card reader beeped as Miranda swiped her ID card over it. The door slid open.

Inside, it was clinically clean, with only a metal table and a high-school-style locker against the far wall. A control panel full of buttons was attached to a bulletproof glass window. Below them was the Exercise Room.

They had a front-row seat to this training exercise.

Tom put the weighty files on the table.

"Are the test subjects fully prepared?" he asked.

"Yes sir. They've been given battle gear, night vision goggles and AK-47s."

"Any secondary weapons?"

"A .44 Magnum side-arm," Miranda said.

"All right. Let the games begin. Bring them in."

Miranda pressed a red button on the control panel.

A door to the far right of the Exercise Room slid up. Ted Morrison, Matt Smyth and Hannah Montrose entered. As they walked in, fluorescent sensor lights came on overhead. Each subject wore army fatigues with a green tactical carrier, shoulder pads and soft-armor ballistic inserts.

The door slid down once they were inside.

"I think it's time we introduce ourselves," Tom said.

"Sir, I have to remind you that anonymity is a must at all times," Miranda told him.

"I know that. I meant metaphorically."

Miranda pressed an orange button to switch on the PA system, and Tom bent down to speak into the microphone.

"Good evening. You've been selected, out of thousands, to perform a top-secret mission to test a new weapon we're about to release. As part of your agreements, Mr. Smyth and Ms. Montrose: if you both pass this, you're a free man and woman. No more jail time, as promised."

"And if we don't?" Hannah shouted.

"Then it's back to prison."

"What about me?" Ted shouted.

"You, Mr. Morrison, will be handsomely rewarded."

"Define 'handsomely'?"

"Enough to buy more than one house."

"Suits me," Ted replied with a broad grin.

"We'll start by seeing how good a shot you are."

Tom gestured with his head to Miranda. She flicked a switch.

The left wall rose up. Behind it were numerous targets in the form of cardboard cutouts, depicting stereotypical terrorists, armed thieves, and people dressed in everyday attire.

"You got twenty seconds to hit as many of the targets as you can. Be careful—some of them are innocent bystanders. Shoot those and you're eliminated. One last thing: those are live rounds in your gun, so be careful. The fun ... starts ... *now.*"

A light came on over the cardboard figures, which moved forward. Ted, Matt and Hannah started shooting, each taking care to not shoot a civilian. A screen to the right of Tom and Miranda monitored the subjects' progress.

A klaxon sounded that their time was up.

"Well done," Tom announced. "You all did very well. Now for the real test." He took his finger off the PA button.

144

"Kill the lights," he said to Miranda.

She did so.

"Whoa, what the hell's goin' on?" Hannah yelled.

Tom spoke again into the microphone. "Put on your goggles."

The targets retreated behind the wall and then it slid down. Shafts opened up on the floor. Seven-foot-high metal barriers, three inches thick, slid up, dividing the room into sections and turning it into a maze.

"My final piece of advice is keep your wits about you. When the siren goes off, you're going green. Watch your backs. Good luck." Tom removed his finger from the button once more. "Bring up Angelina."

"Yes, General," Miranda said.

An image of a tall, broad, human-cat hybrid appeared on the screen. She had peachy skin; long, plaited red hair; and chestnut-brown human eyes. And, while she lacked a tail, much of her face was composed of feline features. A black bulletproof vest covered her upper torso. It was the only item of clothing Angelina wore, save for the metal brace around her neck.

"Are comms working?" Tom asked.

"Yes. We finished putting them into the brace yesterday."

"And she'll understand what I'm saying?"

"Yes sir."

"All right. Turn them on and patch me through," Tom ordered.

As Miranda flipped another switch, a green light blinked on the hybrid's brace.

"Angelina, I want you to kill everyone in that room. Spare no-one. Do you understand that order?" Tom asked.

Angelina grunted, nodding once.

"That seems like a 'yes' to me. Sound the siren and release her," Tom ordered.

"Yes, sir—but before I do, we need these." Miranda opened a locker, retrieving two pairs of night vision goggles. She handed one to Tom. "The lights in this room will go off too once she's out there."

"Good." Tom slid the goggles onto his head and over his eyes.

"All right. Let's not keep them waiting."

Miranda pressed another two buttons. A red siren flashed and blared for half a minute, lighting up the dark Exercise Room.

A side door, out of the test subjects' line of sight, slid open. Angelina crawled out in a crouching predatory stance, seeking her first target. She moved along the wall closest to her. The hybrid's nails transformed into claws that were over an inch long.

All three subjects moved around the mini maze, sweeping their surroundings, swinging their assault rifles left and right. Matt hugged one of the corners, keeping the gun close to his chest. He spun around with his weapon aimed high. Nothing appeared to be there ... until a shadow moved from above.

He couldn't pull the trigger in time. Angelina jumped on him, covering his mouth while slashing his throat with her sharp claws. Blood sprayed across her face and onto the nearby surfaces.

Is she going to take his AK-47? Tom wondered.

Angelina didn't. Instead, she inched to the edge of another wall.

Two targets remained.

Tom saw Angelina paying close attention to Ted, who was the closest. She jumped onto the wall, hopped across another two, and dropped down silently.

Ted walked cautiously, peering around, keeping a tight hold of his weapon. Just as he was about to turn, where Angelina hid, she pounced on him from behind. Sensing her presence, Ted pressed the trigger. There was a short burst of gunfire before Angelina snapped his neck.

The last dance should be interesting, Tom thought.

Hannah, hearing the shooting, scrambled to one of the actual walls, gaining a vantage point in order to see whatever was in there with them.

"Ted, Matt, come in. Do you read me?" she whispered. "Guys, are you there?" she asked again, this time an octave higher.

"Screw this!" Hannah ran through the maze, banging on the door. "Let me out. I'm done. Send me back to me prison. I don't care. Just let me out!"

146

Angelina made her way through the labyrinth until she stopped several feet away from the woman.

Hannah screamed, recoiling, almost dropping her weapon.

"Wha—What?! I don't know what the hell you are." Bringing up the assault rifle, she put Angelina in her sights, curling a finger around the trigger, about to squeeze, "But I'm gonna send you back to hell where you belong!"

Angelina reached out her arm, making a bending motion.

Hannah gasped as the nozzle of her gun was bent down. She dropped it in shock.

Arching back her neck, Angelina let loose a ferocious roar which reverberated around the room. Even Miranda jumped.

Angelina ran towards Hannah, who picked up the AK-47 and threw it at the oncoming monster, hitting Angelina's face. This was enough of a distraction to allow Hannah to draw the .44 Magnum. She got in three shots, bringing Angelina down.

Hannah stood there a moment, panting. She aimed the .44 at Angelina as she walked closer. She stood over the beast, training the weapon at its head.

"I'd like to see you get up after this."

Hannah fired.

A bullet spat out of the gun but stopped an inch from Angelina's brows.

Hannah jumped as Angelina opened her eyes. She fired twice; but once again, the bullets halted in mid-air. Hannah gasped as they changed direction, turning toward her. She dropped her gun, fleeing to the door.

As the bullets fell, Angelina leapt on her prey's back, tearing out Hannah's trachea.

"Impressive. She did well," Tom remarked. "That new vest is incredible."

"Thank you, sir," Miranda replied. "We combined the material with metals we found in a downed UFO. Worked on it for ten weeks until we got the combination right."

"The results speak for themselves. Lights up."

The darkness was banished as both rooms were illuminated.

147

Tom took off his goggles and shook Miranda's hand. "Congratulations, Dr. Hodges. Well done. Send Angelina back to her cage and get the mop-up crew in here."

"Yes. Thank you, General."

***

Ten minutes later, Tom was back in his office, typing an entry into a secret diary on a heavily encrypted laptop. He was pleased with Angelina's progress, and he hoped that within the next six months they could send her out on missions, starting with small fish like killing the leaders of Mexican drug cartels. From there, they'd approach bigger targets. Now that their scientists had discovered the perfect cloning technique, the possibilities were endless.

The sudden sound of a siren blaring made him jump. His mobile phone vibrated—Tom had put it on silent as he didn't want to be disturbed while writing the entry. Miranda's name was on the screen.

"Dr. Hodges, what's wrong?"

"We have a situation, sir." These were the words that he'd always dreaded hearing. "Angelina has escaped."

Tom sat up straight. She had his full attention now. "How the hell did that happen?" he barked.

"She somehow managed to steal a key card from one of the guards and knocked him out."

"Wait a second, are you telling me that she beat all four of her escorts unconscious?"

"No, sir—only two of them. The others were killed."

"Get three teams on her, pronto. I want her brought back to this base immediately! I'll see you in the Situation Room in two minutes." Tom hung up and turned off his laptop.

When he exited the elevator, three armed guards were waiting for him. They saluted as he approached and followed him while he made his way to the Situation Room.

Tom strode in, swinging the door wide.

There were five technicians at their desks, wearing headsets and staring intently at their computers.

Miranda stood in front of a large screen, which was divided into two. Names and photos of every member of the search teams, along with their vitals, were on the right, for now all in green. On the left was a live feed.

"Report," Tom snapped.

"Air teams have found her, sir," said Miranda. "Ground forces are advancing on her location."

"Good. Are those special tranqs we worked on ready?"

"Yes. All the soldiers have them."

"I want Angelina brought back alive if possible." He turned to the techs. "Which of you are comms?"

Two techs raised their hands.

"I want you to patch through this message: 'Use non-lethal force if possible. I want her back alive.' Do it, now," Tom growled.

Both typed furiously before relaying the order on their headsets.

"Which team is that footage from?" he asked Miranda.

"Beta."

"Can we switch between them? I presume they're wearing body cams."

"Yes, sir." Miranda checked the screen for a moment before continuing. "Beta's leader is Captain Burke. Omega's led by Major Connell."

"All right. Let's see who gets her first."

"We got a message from Beta," an auburn-haired tech informed Tom. "They got a visual."

Captain Burke's feed soon confirmed this. He stood behind some foliage, from where only part of Angelina could be seen. She was crouched in an attack pose. She growled, sensing the soldiers' presence.

"Captain Burke is requesting permission to fire," the tech said.

Before Tom could answer, Angelina pounced on a soldier who emerged from the bushes. She made short work of him, ripping through his throat.

Captain Burke and the others didn't wait for permission.

Tom reckoned twenty tranq darts found their way into Angelina's arms and legs. Some also hit her neck.

For a brief moment, Angelina stood defiant, roaring at the soldiers, arms back and claws extended. Then she staggered to her left, taking another two clumsy steps to the right before falling down.

"Careful," Tom mumbled, wondering if this was some trap to lure them in, striking when their guard was lowered.

Captain Burke led his team, his weapon trained on Angelina. He nudged her with his foot. There was no response. He tried another two times, again with the same reaction.

"Captain Burke says she's out," the tech said.

"I can see that. Is the extraction helicopter on the way?"

"Yes sir. ETA 50 seconds," Miranda replied.

"Good. Tell both teams to hold their position and secure the asset until the chopper arrives. She mustn't be allowed to escape again."

"Yes sir," both techs answered in unison.

"Good work, guys. Pass on my congrats to the troops out there. I want to see Captain Burke and Major Connell in my office when they come back. Oh, and Dr. Hodges, make sure something like this doesn't ever happen again. If it does, I'll see to it that you're permanently banned from working in any government position. Understood?"

"Fully sir. I'll put extra contingencies in place to make sure she doesn't get away from us in future."

"See that you do. I'm going to my office. Let me know when Angelina's back in her cell."

"I will, General," Miranda said, browbeaten, unable to meet his gaze.

Tom refilled his cup with freshly brewed tea and sat down at his desk. He was about to put the finishing touches to the diary entry when the phone rang again. He picked it up without looking at the number and pressed the green button.

"What's wrong now?" he barked.

"General Beckford, this is Eagle."

Tom recognized the codename instantly. It was the President of the United States. Mortified, he cleared his throat and changed his cross tone. "Oh, uh, sorry, sir. I thought you were someone else."

"At ease, General. I heard you had a little problem earlier."

"Yes, sir, but it has been contained."

"That's good to hear. I needn't remind you that hundreds of millions of dollars have been pumped into this project." The president's voice now became firmer and more insistent. "I don't want any screw-ups, just so we're clear."

"Oh, I understand, sir. I'm well aware of the amount of money that's been given to us."

"I'm pleased to hear that." Eagle's tone was relaxed and cordial again. "I've been hearing reports that the local PD has received complaints from people about sirens going off and exercise drills. We'll need to move this operation somewhere else. We can't have it compromised now."

"Don't worry, sir, it's being taken care of," Tom assured him.

"So you've found a suitable location?"

Tom spun the globe on the table until it came to America. He tapped his finger on a remote, small town. He grinned with immense pride when he said, "Yes sir. I've already found the perfect place, and construction has begun."

Interview with Aidan Lucid

Thank you for joining us today.

Thanks for having me.

So, this is the end of book three in the series. How does it feel?

Oh, it feels fantastic. These characters took on a life of their own and drove the story in a direction I didn't anticipate. So when *Dark Secrets* ended the way it did, I was kind of shocked, but also excited to see what's in store for the final book of the series, *Lurking Beasts*. There are two kinds of writers: "pantsers" and "plotters". I'm very much a plotter, and have a structured outline; but every once in a while, characters deviate from the "script", so to speak. While I do have an outline and plan for the final book in the *Hopps Town* series, the characters could do something unexpected when I begin writing it.

Are you happy with fans' reactions to the *Hopps Town* series so far?

Yes, definitely. The reaction has been mostly positive, and I appreciate all the support. Some readers say that *The Scavenger* and *Unlucky Charm* are inspirational and give them hope, which is something I always try to do.

How do you think readers will react to *Dark Secrets'* ending, since this is a set of books dealing with the paranormal?

Well, the last thing I wanted to do was to make Jared's adventures formulaic. I didn't want to churn out the same kind of story all the time. With every entry into the *Hopps Town* series, I wanted to try something new and fresh. So, with *Lurking Beasts*, I want to head in a slightly different direction. There will still be some spooky goings on, but I think—and hope—that fans will appreciate the new approach while still staying true to the characters.

Did you always intend to write four books?

No. When I wrote *The Scavenger*, it was only supposed to be a once-off. I wrote that novella's ending in such a way that if the reader reaction/reviews were positive, then I could write another. When I was plotting *Unlucky Charm*, ideas for a further two books came into my head, so I jumped down that "rabbit hole", so to speak, to see where it would lead me.

In a previous interview, you stated that the name "Hopps Town" was inspired by a *Stranger Things* character. Is that true?

Yes, that's correct. My wife and I are big fans of that Netflix show. In particular, we love David Harbour's character, Sherriff Hopper, so I named Jared's hometown in his honor.

Are any of the characters based on you or someone you know?

Not really. Jared is someone I can relate to. When we first meet him in *The Scavenger*, he was kind of unsure of himself and his place in this world, although he had the courage to come out and be himself. In a lot of ways, I can relate to that. For a long time, even though I was fortunate to grow up in a place where people were very understanding and kind, I did face discrimination, and sometimes ridicule, over my disability outside of my hometown. People just take one look at a person and make an unfair judgement. Over the years, I've learned to cope with this in my own way. I have also been very lucky to have such a loving and supportive family and group of friends who believed in me when there were times I didn't have faith in myself. That's why I created Jessica and Adrian. They're Jared's rocks, and will always have his back no matter how dire the situation is.

Is there a possibility of a fifth adventure for Jared and his friends?

Not right now. But as the saying goes, "never say never".

Was there any novel or author you drew inspiration from for any of the _Hopps Town_ titles?

In some ways, I was inspired by Stephen King's, _It._ I loved the dynamic and bond between the kids—the characters and their friendships felt so real. That was something I wanted to incorporate into _The Scavenger_ and the other titles. Apart from that, the question that starts a lot of stories, "What if?", ran across my mind. I thought: "What if three teens, who each have a troubled past or present, made a wish at a cursed well? What would happen then?" So that's how I got the ball rolling on that book.

Your work, for the most part, has received positive reviews. How do you deal with negative ones?

I respect everybody's opinion. Even in the worst review, there is always something to be gleaned or taken away from it that I could improve upon. Some writers state that you shouldn't read them, but I disagree. Not every reader is going to like your story/stories. That's just part of reality. My advice to new authors is to not take the one- or two-star ratings to heart, but read through them. If there's an element of truth in what that reader says, then take that on board and work on it. The one thing you don't do is let that person put you off writing again. Being an author is a lonely, and sometimes unappreciated, job. Just like all professions, one takes the good with the bad. But I wouldn't trade this wonderful job for anything else in the world.

In 2021, you co-wrote a screenplay, *The Haunting of the Scavenger*, with Gary Revel, which is the film adaptation of *The Scavenger*. How's that movie coming along?

It's a slow process, but the movie's coming along nicely. I can't say too much right now, but there'll be some *very* interesting updates on that soon. If people follow me on Twitter (https://twitter.com/TheZargothian), Instagram (https://www.instagram.com/aidanlucidauthor/) and Facebook (https://www.facebook.com/Aidan-Lucids-Books-and-Art-Page-105238694758613), they'll get all the latest news on that there.

So what's next for Aidan Lucid? What other books can we expect?

I hope to release *Deadly Pursuits,* book two in the *Zargothian Saga* series in November 2023. I find writing novellas more fun and productive because it takes nearly half the time of writing a 70,000 word novel. So for now, I will continue to work on novellas. Within the next twelve months, there will be another release of a stand-alone horror novella, *A Beast Within*. There may be a possibility of me branching out into writing screenplays and comic book scripts in the future. For now, however, I'm sticking with writing novellas/short fiction.

Is there anything else you want to add?

Not to sound like a broken record, but I just want to thank everyone who have bought my books and to those who have left a review, too, over the years. From the bottom of my heart, I'm so grateful. It means a lot to me. Us writers wouldn't be able to keep writing without your support. So, again, thank you—or as we say in Irish, "Go raibh mile maith agat" (a thousand thank yous). At this moment, I want to thank my team of beta readers and my extremely talented editor, Megan Openshaw. You're all a Godsend and I'm so blessed to have such wonderful people to work with!

The Scavenger

Just like Hopps Town, their humble home, Jessica Barlow, Jared Duval, and Adrian Cole are fostering dark secrets. Plagued by loss, cruelty, and physical abuse, these friends are kindred spirits, bound by anguish and elusive dreams. They're soon to find the key to change, but any happy future will demand they face a haunting past and brave a lethal present.

Deep in the forest on the outskirts of town, aging and nearly forgotten, there stands a well from another time. Happening upon this relic, Adrian goads his companions to join him in making a wish. Soon, difficult though it is to admit, their luckless lives do seem to shift. The only problem is, the changes aren't at all as they'd imagined. Seemingly, they've only left the pan to face the fire.

Should they hope to both survive and thrive, they'll need to pool their wits and draw on mystic inner-power. Solving Hopps Town's greatest mystery now means life or death.

"This was a fun YA horror with a fast pace and not too much gore." - Well Worth a Read blog

"Lots of people have played with the "magical wish gone wrong" idea, but Lucid did it with far more finesse and subtlety than most writers […] I hope Aidan will show us more of these three friends in future stories."
Gilbert M. Stack

Unlucky Charm

Darkness comes from the most unexpected of places!

Following the events of *The Scavenger*, we now find Jared a year later, on a two-week break from college. He thought this would be a relaxing visit home — then it happened, something so dark he felt a strange sense of déjà vu.

Across town we find Reggie Danes and Zane Miller, who've been friends for over ten years. After Zane purchases an antique pocket watch, they suddenly find themselves being taunted by past secrets.

Now they must band together to vanquish the demons which plague their lives. Can life ever return to normal? Will the darkness ever disappear?

"If you are a horror story enthusiast, grab your copy now!"
Write_Reads

"*Unlucky Charm* is perfect for readers who enjoy high-stakes stories with suspense and scares."
Priscilla Bettis

The Lost Son (Second Edition)

A Magic Coin. A Hidden World. An Incredible Adventure!

Henry Simmons is your average seventeen year old kid, until one day he isn't.

All Henry cares about is gaming and ogling his long-time crush, Tracey Maxwell. It feels to him that the universe has granted his wishes when he stumbles upon a mysterious gold coin in his family's garden.

From manipulating physical objects, to getting Tracey to go to prom with him, Henry basks and revels in the power he believes the coin has granted him. Until one day he finds himself mystically transported to an entirely new dimension, a realm of war and bloodshed.

Henry's life takes a 180, as he is trapped in this dimension and given the responsibility in helping to save its people from King Zakarius and his bloodthirsty Sadarkian army. He must fight for the humans in this realm alongside the human king, or he stands to lose his life and his way back home.

While Henry is burdened with this ambiguous task, he makes a few unexpected allies, from former World War II pilots to his neighbor's cat who can now talk. Will Henry and his little troop defeat King Zakarius's army, or will they fail and be trapped in this strange world forever?

"The Lost Son was written by Aidan Lucid; and, let me tell you, he is going to be one of the shining stars in the literary world."
   - Randy Belaire, author of, "The Reckoning: Chronicles of the Shadow Chaser"

The Lost Son (Second Edition) Audiobook

A Magic Coin. A Hidden World. An Incredible Adventure!

Henry Simmons is your average seventeen year old kid, until one day he isn't.

All Henry cares about is gaming and ogling his long-time crush, Tracey Maxwell. It feels to him that the universe has granted his wishes when he stumbles upon a mysterious gold coin in his family's garden.

From manipulating physical objects, to getting Tracey to go to prom with him, Henry basks and revels in the power he believes the coin has granted him. Until one day he finds himself mystically transported to an entirely new dimension, a realm of war and bloodshed.

Henry's life takes a 180, as he is trapped in this dimension and given the responsibility in helping to save its people from King Zakarius and his bloodthirsty Sadarkian army. He must fight for the humans in this realm alongside the human king, or he stands to lose his life and his way back home.

While Henry is burdened with this ambiguous task, he makes a few unexpected allies, from former World War II pilots to his neighbor's cat who can now talk. Will Henry and his little troop defeat King Zakarius's army, or will they fail and be trapped in this strange world forever?

"The Lost Son was written by Aidan Lucid; and, let me tell you, he is going to be one of the shining stars in the literary world."
    - Randy Belaire, author of, "The Reckoning: Chronicles of the Shadow Chaser"

About the Author

Aidan Lucid began writing in 2002 after having a spiritual experience. Since then, his works have appeared in national and international poetry anthologies, magazines and e-zines. Lucid first began working on *The Zargothian Saga* trilogy while recovering from a horrific accident in 2005.

Aidan released *The Scavenger* — a horror novella — in January 2021. The first book in the *Hopps Town* series, it received many positive reviews. He followed that up with *Unlucky Charm* in January 2022.

Mr. Lucid is working on more sequels to *The Zargpthian Saga* and stand-alone horror novellas.

In his spare time he likes to meditate, listen to music and go to the movies with his wife, Claire.

Did you enjoy the book?

So, what did you think of, *Dark Secrets*? Did you like/dislike it? I'd love to hear your thoughts by you posting a review. Each one helps get a book noticed; but it also tells an author what he or she is doing right or wrong, so they can improve their future books. At the end of the day, us authors want to please you guys, the readers. So, please leave a review.

Thank you.

Join My Mailing List

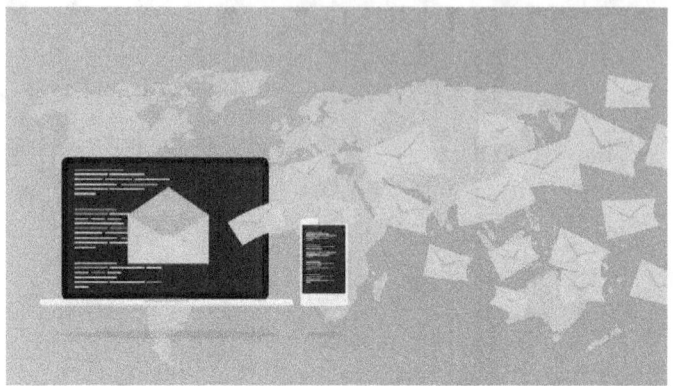

Be sure to sign up to my mailing list today to be notified of the following:

- Upcoming releases
- Free ebook offers
- Ebook discounts and special price promotions
- Competitions
- New merchandise

Visit this link to subscribe: https://www.subscribepage.com/hopps_town_mailinglist

Connect with Aidan on:

 https://twitter.com/TheZargothian

 https://www.instagram.com/aidanlucidauthor/

 https://www.facebook.com/adian.lucid.7

www.ingramcontent.com/pod-product-compliance
Lightning Source LLC
Chambersburg PA
CBHW071523170626
46811CB00007B/2935